TO HAVE AND TO HOLD

The Yorkshire Saga Series Book Three

Valerie Holmes

Also in the Yorkshire Saga Series
To Love, Honour and Obey
For Richer, For Poorer

TO HAVE AND TO HOLD

Published by Sapere Books.

20 Windermere Drive, Leeds, England, LS17 7UZ, United Kingdom

saperebooks.com

Copyright © Valerie Holmes, 2019
Valerie Holmes has asserted her right to be identified as the author of this work.
All rights reserved.

No part of this publication may be reproduced, stored in any retrieval system, or transmitted, in any form, or by any means, electronic, mechanical, photocopying, recording, or otherwise, without the prior written permission of the publishers.
This book is a work of fiction. Names, characters, businesses, organisations, places and events, other than those clearly in the public domain, are either the product of the author's imagination, or are used fictitiously.
Any resemblances to actual persons, living or dead, events or locales are purely coincidental.

ISBN: 978-1-913028-01-5

Prologue

Garebeck Mill, North Riding of Yorkshire
September 1st 1819

"Jebediah Flitch! Jebediah Flitch! Where are you, you lazy wretch?" The voice of the overseer of the mill bellowed out of his twisted mouth.

"Where's Jeb?" whispered a raggedy boy to another shuffling along next to him. His breath dispersed as vapour on the air and he shoved his cold hands deep into his pockets.

The children were answering the roll call for the start of another twelve-hour shift. It was still dark and their long day would not end till after the sun that was yet to rise had set. The other lad shrugged, digging his clenched fists deeper into the pockets of his old trousers, his downcast eyes staring at the ill-fitting boots tied on with string that slipped and flopped around his feet loosely; he would grow into them, he had been told.

The boys made their way inside the factory doors before the bell finished ringing. The dew formed an ice-like covering over the old cobblestones.

"He's done a runner!" bellowed the formidable figure of Mrs Cookson as she came out of the school room. "He should have been here an hour since as punishment for falling asleep in me lessons yesterday evening, but instead he's up and gone." She glared at the approaching children as they passed by her door.

"He was hurt yesterday, Mrs Cookson," a young girl, Esther, chirped up.

The sharp thwack of Mrs Cookson's hand on the lass's cheek seemed to echo in the resounding silence. The children were instructed only to answer when spoken to. It was one of many rules, and breaking any of them, no matter how small, resulted in an instant, harsh punishment.

"Who gave you permission to speak out?" Mr Bullman, the overseer, barked.

Esther looked tearfully back at him but did not voice anymore thoughts.

"Well, what if he was?" Mrs Cookson rounded on the girl, whose hands were shaking, eyes fighting to hold back unshed tears as she pulled her tattered woollen shawl around her thin body. "We all get hurt at times, but work is work and has to be done! You set them men of yours looking for him, Mr Bullman. They like a chase and that little brat won't get far, not with his cuts and bruises."

Jeb's friends looked at each other and then stared at the ground as they stepped inside the gates. He was in trouble, but there was nothing they could do. It was hard enough looking out for each other in the mill, but out there were moors and highwaymen and smugglers, and worse — hobgoblins.

Mr Bullman waved the children onward and into the mill.

"Aye, we'll catch him and his will be a lesson you'll all remember," he yelled over their heads as they disappeared into the noisy, clattering building. This was their dust laden place of warmth until they crossed back over the cold yard for their supper and lesson before crashing onto their dormitory mattresses for a few hours' precious sleep. "We provide a home here for you, and yet some of you are so lazy that you don't want to do an honest day's work to keep the mill going. Think on that young fool, Jebediah Flitch. He's set his path and it will not end happily… You can take my word on that!"

Chapter 1

Laura Pennington skipped down the stairs and cut through the kitchens, grabbing a slab of parkin on her way, stopping only long enough to drink a fresh glass of milk prepared for her mama's waking. The servants, busy at their chores, hardly noticed her as she slipped down the corridor between the laundry and the cold store. Only Mabel, the cook, saw her take the drink and shook her head, but Laura saw the smile on her lips and knew that she would not say a word to her mama.

Today, Laura was going to defy the Hamiltons on behalf of the local people, by walking the path of her childhood. The land it crossed was now part of the Hamilton estate, and they had enclosed a section of the majestic headland of Stangcliffe, or at least the path leading to it. Laura felt alive and a thrill of excitement swept through her as it had as a child when she could run free along the sweeping bay all the way from the southernmost point, Stangcliffe, to Gannet Rock at the northern end of the flat sandy beach.

From Ebton to Alunby, the small fishing villages of generations past were changing as the new roads brought strangers into the area, and buildings, finer and grander than the small cruck-built cottages of the old villages, were being developed. Laura ran out of the back of one of the fine crescents of new homes, down into the valley of the gill. Here she followed the path that skirted the tributary when it was not in fast flow after heavy rain. She crossed its course by the steppingstones and carried on up the steep woodland path onto the Hamiltons' land at the southern side. This sheltered enclave had been protected from the elements by its steep sides. In May, the smell of wild garlic flowers would have enticed her, but today she had brought a small broad bladed knife to unearth some of the hidden bulbs. Her mother used to swear by them for the treatment of colds in winter. Laura collected them, along with wild blackberries in her basket as she went. The day was young and it was all hers.

Mr Obadiah Pennington's heart filled with pride as he walked over to his row of fishing boats, lined neatly on the beach near the 'Coble Inn'. After inheriting his father's fishing boat he had built up his own little empire. When the smuggling, which had supplemented the townships on this northeast section of coast died out, Obadiah saw the town changing and knew that he had to fill a void, or people would go hungry again, because fish and crops had seasons. One bad season, and the villagers would starve. The money from contraband had kept the local economy afloat and that was now gone, so he had thought fast and he had recreated the town in his mind as he would have it.

New roads had brought strangers nearer. The richer folk were moving down from the colliery towns. They were the owners, the tradesmen, those who built mansions on the backs of the miners' efforts. The towns they established were more crowded and far dirtier than the farming villages many of them grew up in. So they sought out a healthier, fresher climate. Just like the thriving spa towns of Harrogate and Scarborough, Ebton was also becoming a place to bathe and take the fresh air — although it was often quite cold. But even the cold air was supposed to be good for the body as it cleansed the bad humours, or so Obadiah had helped to spread the tales of its miraculous properties far and wide. He knew that a strong conviction could sell a story as much as the smell of a good baker's oven would sell a loaf. He just had to keep the tongues wagging and the visitors fed with well-cooked fresh seafood.

Obadiah saw that where there was a desire, there was also an opportunity to do trade. He had been to Scarborough and had seen an unusual contraption and copied it. He offered the use of Ebton's first bathing machine; this was a success which led to the purchase of three more. Trips out to sea followed, going along the coast to the bay towns further south, when the weather and tide permitted. He filled the trippers' heads with tales of the benefits of eating the freshly caught and dressed Whitby crabs. Then, of course, he led them to a place where catches could be bought fresh from one of his boats, offering to have them cooked for free on their return. It was a clever ruse for it meant they bought their own dinners.

For the more daring he even ran fishing trips. Soon he had five boats and was also running a small respectable hotel in the new part of town run by Mrs Myrtle King, a widowed landlady who ran a clean and friendly house. He had had great ideas beyond the hard and seasonal life of a fisherman. His vision was providing work for many in the communities, along with an ever-growing profit margin. Fishing still had its place, but so did his other ventures.

The sea was calm and stretched out to a grey-green horizon. Trade was brisk from Newcastle and other ports further north, down to the mighty river Thames in the south. Mighty because of its wealth rather than size and due to the prosperity it offered to those wise enough to grow their own trade there. From where he stood next to the original cottages of Ebton, which were almost built upon the beach next to the inn, he glanced up at the line of terraced houses facing the bay on the opposite lower cliff. He admired the result of his vision and steadfast toil that these fine crescent houses represented. Soon this place would have many visitors like the southern town of Scarborough. He hoped that they would draw in a wealthier crowd, encouraging day trippers and families. He even thought of making a spa hotel, if he could only source something that could pass as a natural spring — Harrogate thrived on them, so why not 'Ebton on the Sands'? He glanced back at the Coble Inn and wondered why the ale there still tasted better than anywhere else. Somewhat sheltered from the vast ocean expanse by the imposing headland, he pondered if would survive his plans. Nostalgia had its place, but people and places had to move on, didn't they? Did he care? He shrugged, dismissing thr thoughts that tried to reach down to find his conscience.

A distant figure moving briskly behind the Coble Inn caught his attention and his moment of happiness was instantly cloaked by a veil of anger. "Laura!" he snapped. His daughter, his only child, was walking briskly across the gardens behind the old village where a stream had cut a deep ravine. Obadiah sighed. Her mother for once was quite right; Laura had no sense of how to behave. She was putting herself in danger, and a young lady should not be venturing out on her own. She had to stop thinking like a local lass and consider her reputation, and his.

Obadiah removed his hat and ruffled his greying hair with his fingers; like the rest of his body they were strong through years of hard graft. Laura was totally oblivious to the fact that she was being observed. She was old enough to marry and yet she behaved like a carefree child. His Laura had broken her word to him! She had lied, disobeying his orders not to go to such places. He never would have thought that she would. In that moment something inside him broke; a relationship based upon trust was shattered.

With his wealth and position in the town — no, in all the towns along the bay — she could marry well — into more new money. Her behaviour was careless. Did she not seek to make a good match? Did she want to be a fisherman's wife like her mother and grandmother and the generations afore them? What life would that be for her, and after all he had done to take the family away from that life of endless toil? Yet this was his reward — a stupid, selfish girl!

The last few weeks he had lain awake, pondering how to broach the subject of marriage to her; it was now obvious that the time had arrived. There would be no flighty romance for her with a local lad; he would make sure of that. She would be matched to someone with good prospects. He had two suitors in mind — both mill owners from over the moors. Both men were single, successful, and their cotton mills were within twenty miles of her home. Personally, he preferred the younger Tranton, Daniel He was a fair man and Obadiah respected him, but Obadiah's darling wife, Mrs Gladys Pennington, wanted him to approach Daniel Tranton's elder cousin, Mr Roderick Tranton. His mill was nearer to them, being situated on the outskirts of Gorebeck, only six miles inland. But, Obadiah would rather not see Laura wed to that cold-hearted wimp of a man.

Obadiah had already written to the younger bachelor, asking him to consider settling down with his beautiful, wilful daughter, Laura. He prayed that the man would take the proposition seriously. To add impetus he had also suggested he would be writing to Roderick as an alternative. Daniel was his first choice, but either way, Laura was to marry. He watched her make for the pathway that would lead straight onto the private land to the opposite side of the beck, and realised she was headed for the Hamiltons' estate, another place he had forbidden her to go!

"Obadiah!" The call from a fisherman approaching his boat meant he had to walk away from his vantage point, so Laura would have her way today — for the very last time. The next letter he hoped to receive, and soon, would be one of introduction from Mr Daniel Tranton, making the first step in what he hoped would be a successful and contented union.

Daniel Tranton rode into Gorebeck over the old dry-stone bridge. It still held onto its charm, yet this North Riding market town had grown so much from his boyhood memories of a much quieter village. The Norman church still looked mellow and beautiful as he approached the bridge, but the new housing had all but replaced the cruck-built cottages that had once lined the muddy track leading to the centuries-old market square.

Daniel's mind had been in turmoil ever since he received a most unusual letter from his associate, Mr Obadiah Pennington. His first encounters with Obadiah had been somewhat uneasy, but they had long since become friends, had served together, and now, as a successful mill owner, Daniel had traded and earned a mutual respect from the man. Daniel had learned a lot from Obadiah, beyond what his education in a private school could offer. Pennington had shown him many a harsh life lesson. In exchange, Daniel had helped Obadiah learn his letters — the man already had a natural gift for numbers. Apparently, Daniel had earned more of the man's trust than he realised, as Obadiah's only child was now being offered to him, along with a portion of his trading routes to Holland and France. That was an interesting proposition, except for one slight problem; Daniel had no wish to marry.

But how could he decline the girl without offending her father or risking losing access to the trade route he so desperately needed to build his business up? He relied on the vital link for his mill's cloth to be sold, but if he turned the offer of Laura's hand down then it could go to a competitor.

Daniel's attention was taken by a commotion coming from a group of people gathering outside an ale house. Five men poured out of the Hare and Rabbit, led by a man he knew well — a very angry man. The inn had always been a peaceful place until Ivor Bullman and his men arrived.

"Mr Bullman, what is the trouble here? Has something happened at the mill?" Daniel asked. He was polite but he held no regard for Bullman or his ways. He could not, however, openly disclose his true feelings, as his cousin, Roderick had allowed Bullman, his employee, to gain a position of growing power in the town. Why, Daniel could not understand.

The naked hunger in the group's eyes was almost palpable, and it was a sight Daniel knew well — that hunger for blood.

"Aye, sir, we have a runner. He knew the rules and so has brought his own fate down upon his thick skull, and that cannot go unpunished. We scouted the Beckton area yesterday, but we didn't pick up his trail. We lost it in the woodland."

"Why would you think he would come near to my mill, if he is a runaway?" Daniel asked.

The man shrugged. "You never know how an idiot's mind works. We'll be out again soon and we shall catch the little blighter. You know Mr Roderick's views. Like in the Indies, runners need to be made to appreciate how good their fortune had been!" The man was almost drooling at the prospect of catching the poor lad.

"This is not the Indies, though, and surely those days are now behind us. Jeb is no more than a boy, if I remember him correctly and…"

"Flitch is twelve summers if he is a day! He is old enough to run like a man so he is old enough to stand punishment for it like one. He could have served on a man of war or as a foot soldier by now, so why should he be treated as a child?" The man sniffed and wiped his nose on the back of his sleeve.

Daniel looked down at this group of men. They were Bullman's usual heavies, who would have done well as a pressgang, Daniel thought. Roderick would reward them with extra ale if they found the lad. His cousin believed that these returning soldiers were loyal to their country, and therefore would be loyal to him also if he let them run the mill. In Daniel's eyes, the only loyalty they had was to themselves and they were perfect examples of Wellington's 'scum of the earth', who had returned true to type. He suspected they were bleeding Roderick dry, but Daniel could not prove it. He wanted to talk to his cousin about it, but Roderick insisted that, as the elder, he was also the wiser cousin. The phrase 'no fool like an old one' came to Daniel's mind.

"When did he run?" Daniel asked.

"Night before last, but he won't get far 'cos he's injured. Bloody careless he was, nearly broke the machine he was working with. Well, when we catch him he'll be lucky not to have a broken neck, eh?" Bullman laughed.

Daniel didn't.

"Excuse me, sir, no time for dithering."

Daniel breathed deeply as he watched the group mount their horses. He had to find Jeb, and quickly.

"Has nobody seen him?" Daniel called after them.

"Nope. He took off some time in the middle of the night. I reckon we'll have him back before the day's out. He's had a day's grace to think about his folly, on an empty belly, too." Bullman touched his tattered tall hat and waved his hand forward. "Come on, lads. He's wounded prey; we'll be drinking our fill again in no time."

They laughed at the prospect and rode at a pace up the newly surfaced road and headed out of the town.

Daniel had been on his way to see Roderick to discuss the public meeting that was being planned by the mill workers in the area, but the words 'he's wounded prey' lingered in his mind. Jeb was a good lad; Daniel had seen him at the mill many times. The lad loved horses and had happily seen to Daniel's on his infrequent visits. Where would the lad have gone? He had to set off in the same direction as Jeb to get a head start on the other men.

Daniel dismounted and headed into the inn. He sat on the settle by the bay window where he could keep a watchful eye on the road should the men return. The serving girl, May had seen him enter and her eyes were noticeably moist as she walked over to him.

"They're hunting Jeb?" she asked quietly. Daniel had seen how close May and Jeb were from the day Jeb entered the mill. May had adopted him as a younger brother and it was plain that the two isolated children had found joy in each other's company. May had also been a child of the mill, but on her last birthday she had been offered work at the Inn and had left that life for one not much improved, but perhaps one that would give her a better chance to find a husband.

"Yes, that is why I came in here, May. Can you tell me where he went? I have to find him if he is going to escape their punishment." Daniel looked into her concerned eyes, her hand trembling as she picked up an empty tankard.

She made to brush down the crumbs from the table with her cloth and nodded, barely able to hold back her tears.

"Help me, May, and I will find a way to save your friend. He is a good lad and I know you are fond of him. Trust me for Jeb's sake," he added. "I am the only one who is prepared to help him against Bullman's henchmen."

"They're heading for the open moor, thinking he wants to hitch a ride to York or Whitby. You know, as if he would be thinking to lose himself in the port or city, but he won't because he'd be too far off." She was speaking quietly and glancing anxiously around her.

She went and served someone else and then returned to Daniel, making sure that no one could overhear their conversation.

"Where would he go instead?"

"To the sea, sir," she sniffed. "He's got a cut arm, though, and he might… I mean it might..." May swallowed and turned to clear another table before finishing her sentence. "His arm needs more help than I could give it, but he wants to go on the sea, and breathe fresh air again…" She shook her head. "Oh, sir, whatever is to become of him?"

"Dreams, pipe dreams. The sea is a cruel mistress. This wound, though, do you think that could kill him if left untended?"

She nodded and swallowed.

"Thank you, May. I'll see if I can pick up his trail." Daniel stood up.

"Sir, you won't bring him back here, will you? I mean, Mr Roderick'll have him publicly beaten for this. His character may be strong, but Jeb's body is slight. He desperately needs help." She swallowed again and closed her eyes for a brief moment.

"I give you my word that I will see him safe. If he has a crime to answer for, it will be dealt with by a kindly eye, but if he has been wronged, then I will bring him before my cousin myself and see fair and equitable justice is done." Daniel patted her shoulder as he walked by.

Shyly, May nodded in gratitude.

Daniel left the town, heading up to the moor road, but then his heart sank as he realised May was wrong. Bullman had also headed across the old monks' trods to the coast. They must have picked up on the lad's trail.

"Damnation!" Daniel swore. He had made a promise to the lass and he would keep it, but he was going to have to outwit a group of seasoned ex-soldiers, who had few morals and far fewer scruples.

Chapter 2

Laura shielded her eyes with her bonnet as she looked out at the view of the sea. Ebton had grown and changed so much since she was a small child. Laura's family had once lived in one of the small fishermen's cottages near the beach. They were simple abodes, very different to the new stone-built houses on the opposite lower cliff where they lived now. Laura still yearned for her old home, its nearness to the elements and the strong community that had existed there. She now seemed a stranger to her childhood neighbours, which made her sad. There had been always gossip, shouting, singing or something going on — the old village was alive and vibrant and she wanted to be a part of that, not cosseted in the new house with her mother.

She watched a plume of smoke from one of the cottage's chimneys and remembered the disaster fifteen years ago when one had gone up in flames. It had nestled behind the small Methodist chapel, and the whole village could have vanished had it not been for the quick-thinking inhabitants. Luckily, people had been up and about already and, making use of the seawater, they had saved Ebton from becoming ashes. Word had it that an infamous gang of smugglers was broken up the night of the fire, and the tales her grandpa had told her about them had captivated her young mind, fanning a desire to do more in life than embroidery and lessons — she wanted to feel that same childhood excitement of being barefoot on the beach, running in and out of the waves.

The sense of danger in trespassing on the Hamiltons' estate was exhilarating, and appealed to her restless nature. Laura was a survivor — it was her father's legacy to her; to be able to think her way out of difficulty. He had survived the press gangs, the smugglers, had seen his moment of opportunity and acted, and because of this the family had thrived, as he was now a respectable businessman. Laura wondered sometimes, though, if her father also missed the old cottage and running and playing with her on the beach.

She smiled as she watched the fishing boats being brought up onto the beach, laden with their catch. One was preparing to leave. She could not tell who was on it, but it looked to be one of her father's cobles. He would be furious with her if he knew where she was, but he was always too busy to care these days. That was the sad truth of it — he simply did not have time for her.

Laura stared at the sea's mesmerising beauty, watching the activity upon it: a myriad of vessels making their way up and down the coast, from London to Newcastle and foreign lands far off. She breathed in, wondering what it would be like to set sail across the vast expanse of water, a dot on the edge of violent waves one moment and in the swell of a calm flowing ocean the next, beyond control and at the mercy and will of nature.

Lost to her thoughts, Laura carelessly tripped over a small branch. The basket she was carrying fell to the ground next to her. She now had a mark on her skirts. She bent double to try and brush away the soil from the fabric without smudging it further, but fell to the ground as a pistol shot rang out above her head. It had come through the woodland. Quickly, her basket discarded, Laura leaned back against the relatively smooth bark of an ash tree, listening intently to try and determine what was happening.

It had been foolish to enter the woodland on her own, and she had been stupid enough to risk being caught. Why? So that she could make a stand and enjoy the wild blackberries, as the locals had for years before the Hamiltons' fences arrived? She had wanted to make a point, like the men and women had who had died in Peterloo a few weeks ago. She had read the report out to her father when the newspapers had arrived. Who would have thought that English soldiers — yeomanry, hussars, and cavalry — would hack into a crowd of their own countrymen? It made a mockery of the wars with France. The government feared a revolution, and Laura felt that all the fear, the wars, the poverty that had resulted, were fuelling a mania throughout the country. Most people just wanted food in their bellies and peace; a time for families to reunite and grow strong again. How could the army turn on its own people?

Laura flinched as another shot rang out, only nearer this time. She let out a stifled scream as it splintered a branch on a tree opposite her. This was too close. She either ran for her life or risked being shot. The sense of danger she had craved was now only too real.

Voices carried on the light breeze. "That way — get him!"

A hunt was under way, but the noises she was hearing were all human, not the bustling panic of a startled animal, fleeing for its life.

"Over here!" another voice rang out, the accent not quite local. She swallowed. Whoever 'he' was they were too close to Laura for her comfort. She grabbed her basket and ran for dear life. She was trespassing and, looking at the basket filled with the fruits of the forest and wild garlic, she realised that her belief in her right to use nature's free gifts could be construed as theft.

Laura half ran, half slipped down the bank. The level of the water was low, so she reasoned she could follow the course of the stream to get back to the old town, and from there to the safety of her home. It was what the old smugglers in the region had done, and although it was very dangerous if there was a flood, at least it offered a quick way back to Ebton. As she ran away, grateful that she had always been an active child, she realised she could not reveal her adventure without placing herself in a lot of trouble. She had not only gone against her father's orders; she had broken her word to him.

Calming her breathing down, she tried to regain control. Her trembling body steadied until she heard further rustling in the ferns behind her. She panicked and slipped; her long skirt caught on the undergrowth, tugging at brambles and briars. She lost hold of her basket and watched helplessly as it floated away downstream.

Another shot was fired, but this time it appeared to be over the land above her. Relieved that the noise was more distant, she lay still against the bank, her skirt pinning her there.

"Thank God!" she muttered, as she regained her composure and admonished herself for being so careless with the results of her morning's labour. She had risked her safety for nothing. She ran like a coward from an invisible enemy and lost a basket that she had taken great pleasure in making herself.

A noise above her made her grasp frantically at the material of her skirt, trying desperately to free it but, before she could turn, a man slid down the bank next to her. His hand grabbed hers as he descended. His other roughly ripped the material free, bringing some undergrowth with it and making only one small snag its fabric.

Laura pulled away as hard as she could, but he did not stop to introduce himself or explain his actions. Instead of breaking free of his grip, Laura found herself unwittingly running hand in hand with the dark-haired stranger, crossing the gill to the opposite bank. Without pausing, he pulled her up the other side to the path hidden by ancient oak and ash trees. The crack of a distant shot told her that her pursuers had moved further down the woods on the far side. She looked at the stranger's face to catch an unmistakable look of relief upon it. Then he smiled at her as she stared blankly at him, wondering who he was.

Laura tugged her hand from his. She knew a place, behind a large boulder, overgrown by ivy, where she would be hidden from view if she could only break away from him, but not if he watched her slip into it. Desperation and frustration grew as she looked at the stranger; he was staring straight back into her eyes.

"Who are you, sir?" she snapped.

"You must come with me." Ignoring her efforts to pull away, he held her hand firmly, turned and half walked, half dragged her up the path along the gill away from her home.

"Let me go or I will scream and have all the villagers fall upon you, sir!" Laura protested.

"That you will not!" he said back to her as he glanced over his shoulder.

His confidence irritated her.

"I will!" Now she felt even more like a child, expecting him to chunter, 'Will not!' in response.

He stopped. "No, you will not, because you were running, too, and that means you were up to no good. So be silent and come with me without further fuss. I will explain once we are there." He moved away.

"Why should I? Where's there?" Laura said, as she stumbled along behind him, still being led reluctantly by her hand. An image of her father's irate face appeared as a vision before her troubled mind.

"Because I have asked you to and I need your help." He did not slow his pace or explain further.

"You have not asked me at all!" Laura's voice rose.

He spun around and sighed, his deep blue eyes looking at her imploringly. He changed his tone and softened his words. "Very well. Miss, please help me, I have a friend who could be dying as we speak."

At first she thought his words were driven by sarcasm, but soon realised he meant every one of them. "Very well, show me this friend of yours, and then you can explain all quickly, whilst I decide what is to be done."

He nodded, yet still he held on to her as he branched off the path and headed directly for her hidden place behind the large overgrown boulder.

"He's in here," the stranger said, moving the undergrowth aside.

Laura froze, angry that her childhood hiding place had been so easily discovered. She must escape this man's grip. "I am not going in there with you!" She tried to pull free. "Who is 'he', anyway?"

"Miss, we need your help and, seeing as you are running from them, too, I would say that you are the one who has been placed in our path to provide it." He looked behind them, still obviously anxious that their pursuers could have picked up on their trail.

A lock of dark hair fell across his cheek as he paused and waited for her to move forward. It was not exactly anger that Laura read in his expression, but impatience. She had no intention of slipping into a dark cavern with two 'outlaws'. He must think her a complete dimwit.

"No one placed me in your path! And it was you who was running, not I," she added, tilting her head upwards in defiance as she tried to take a step back, but he held her hand firmly.

"Then why did you throw your basket into the water and run for your life down that slope? Do you have such an affinity with the trees that you were resting against them, blending, as it were, with nature? Or were you actually collecting your wits and breath as the hunt ensued around you?"

She glared at his hand as she tried to think of any argument to put forward in defence of her actions, but she could not.

He let go of her and folded his arms across his shirted chest. "I will not apologise to you if that is what you expect when I have clearly rescued you from a fate you would not want explaining. You were hooked to the bank, woman. What do you think would have happened if I had left you there and they had found you?" He shook his head at her and she instantly thought of her father despairing at finding her on her own outside the house again.

She knew this man had seen too much of her actions to lie about what she was doing. That would only add the label of 'liar' to the 'wanton' one he perhaps already had for her. So if she could not cover her behaviour with a credible tale, she would have to bluff her way through this exchange and go as quickly as she could to the claustrophobic safety of her mama's day room.

Laura studied him. He was dressed in fine trousers and boots, running in a shirt that should have been under a decent man's coat. His language was educated, with no hint of a local accent, and his stature bold, but he had been the hunted, not a gentleman hunter. There was no sense to it, but she was intrigued, rather than scared.

"They had already passed me. I would have returned home," she told him.

"Mr Daniel, is that you?" A feeble voice emerged from the gap behind the boulder.

"Shh, boy! Yes it is and I have brought help with me." He raised a brow and stared at Laura.

"Thank you, Mr Daniel!" the voice exclaimed weakly.

"Come into the light so our friend can see you," Daniel said, and Laura watched as a small figure emerged slowly from the shadows. His face was quite gaunt, but his right eye was swollen and his arm was strapped to his side with a belt. Around his shoulders was a coat that was clearly too big for him. Daniel's, Laura presumed, as the older man smiled reassuringly at the lad.

"Who are you?" Laura asked. Her eyes were set on the bruised figure who leaned precariously against the rock in front of her. "Why are you hiding in here?"

"I'm Jeb Flitch, miss. I fled from the mill over at Gorebeck. I was hurt in an accident and they were going to make me go back under the machines and I… I was too scared. They own me and I have run away… I'll be hunted till they get me back. I'll be flogged or .." He trailed off.

"Enough, Jeb, I have found you before them and I made you a promise that I shall keep. But you must rest, stay out of their way and this lady, I believe, will help you. Then I can sort things out so that you do not need to return to that place or spend your life running from them." He looked at Laura's bemused face. "Well, miss, what do you say?"

"Well, what? I do not know who you are, or who you think I am that would make you believe that I can help you." She swallowed as he moved slightly toward her.

"Do not fear me…" he answered her gesture, "I really am trying to help, that is all. I have some influence at the mill, but I need to talk to them before they find the lad and punish him, for I believe they will be harsh. Runners are discouraged and that is why I need to see Mr Roderick Tranton, the owner of the mill first, before Jeb is returned."

"I fear no man!" Laura said in defiance.

"Then you should do, for there are many that are dangerous and would seek to… Especially if they found such a pretty maid pinned to the bank by her raised skirts."

Laura coloured deeply. She had been overtaken by events and had not thought what a sight she must have revealed to this stranger.

"Look, we waste time. Are you onside or not?"

Laura straightened her back to hide the shame that gnawed at her conscience. "Why would they listen to you? What position do you hold? You are also a 'runner', are you not? Or do you normally scurry around in bushes and down banks?"

A flicker of a smile crossed his lips before he calmly explained, "I am the owner's cousin, Mr Daniel Tranton. We have different opinions on some issues and I hope to break his harsh rules and have him allow me to take the boy on at my own mill. Then I can see Jeb work safely, but diligently, to pay off his debt of gratitude for saving his young skin from a thrashing."

Laura stared back at him. "You too are a mill owner? Yet you are chased around the woodland? Why not make a stand and tell them to stop, leave the lad and go back to your cousin?"

Daniel nodded thoughtfully. "If it was that straightforward, do you not think that I would have done it? They have the right to take him as they are under the orders of Roderick to do so. I could merely plead his case when he was returned —

but Jeb needs attention now. He is in no fit state to travel. Will you help him?" he asked.

"I have little enough money to live on. My father is a fisherman and my mother is not from a wealthy family… I cannot do much and you obviously can." Laura wanted to help the boy but her mother would never allow it and her father would be furious that she had gone onto the Hamilton estate.

"If he was a fisherman then you would have fish a-plenty at this time of year. I only ask you keep Jeb's secret here; you clearly have the freedom to wander this area unchaperoned. You also have the knowledge, mind and ability to trespass and collect food, when you do not throw your gatherings to the wind, that is."

Laura found herself trapped by her own actions. If he knew who she was would he appeal to her father? If so, her actions would be known for what they were — disobedient and stupid. Perhaps she should let this man talk to her father. They could both take the boy to him. He would make an excellent distraction.

"He needs a blanket, some food and a place to hide for a few hours until Bullman's men are clear and I can return," Daniel added.

"Why would you trust him to my care?" she asked. Her mind was spinning from trying to comprehend what she was being asked to become involved in. If she took this child in, was she also breaking the law? Yet, if she left him here to be found then she was no better than the man who had injured him, or who sent him back to grovel on the floor collecting bits of cloth and thread from under a machine.

He half smiled at her. "Because, Miss Laura Pennington, I know you are the daughter of Pennington's fisheries and I doubt that Obadiah would see a young lad starve. If he doubts your actions, tell him that Mr Daniel Tranton has placed him in your care. He will not query it."

Laura stared at him in disbelief. How did he know her name, let alone her father's? "How can you speak so? You do not know him ... do you?"

"I cannot be seen in the town here as I should not be involved in this escapade. I must return to the mill and see if I can deal with Roderick. But it is essential they have no knowledge of my involvement at this point. The legal rights are with Roderick and his men and I do not wish to become embroiled in a battle of property between myself and my cousin. We have larger issues to face than the plight of one hapless lad. But that does not mean I will stand by and let him be hunted like a fox. Those men, Miss Pennington, are not gentlemen, they are lowlifes, who have little conscience."

"How do you know my father?" Laura's stern stance seemed to amuse the stranger until he saw the lad beginning to sink at the knees. He scooped him up in his arms as if he weighed no more than a babe. Laura could not fathom how this stranger should speak so informally to her as if they were already familiar acquaintances. She had not even heard his name spoken before. The Gorebeck Mill, though, was known; its reputation was almost as bleak as that of the poor house.

"I will help him, but I cannot carry him. You will have to stay here a while longer. I will go and fetch some food, a blanket and my father, if he has returned. Then, Mr Daniel Tranton, you can explain yourself to him."

"Very well, but, Miss Laura, how will you explain why you were on their land?" he asked.

"That is an issue I will deal with." Laura's confidence returned, for when it came to facing her father, she had no fears. The man was just and, what is more, loved her dearly. He would understand because she shared his spirit. Her mother, however, did not, and she could be a problem.

Daniel nodded and took the lad back inside the shelter of the small cavernous space. "Be quick about it, though, he is cold and hungry."

His voice lingered on the air as she ran down the path and wondered what to tell her father. She did not fear him, but she hated to let him down. Laura's thoughts shook her — she had broken her word to him and that was unforgivable.

Chapter 3

Laura entered her home by the tall green door, newly painted, like everything inside. There were no more stone-flagged floors as in their old cottage; instead they lived in grand style like the townsfolk in the market town of Gorebeck over the moor. The newly laid carpet stretched out before her and the fanlight above the door allowed the sun to shine directly into the painted hallway. The white door surrounds led to four different rooms: blue for the morning room, green for the library, cream for the drawing room and aqua for the dining room. Mrs Gladys Pennington had created her ideal home and no one questioned her taste. Fortunately, she did not have many callers from over the moor who could discern what was apt and what was not. The local people had similar tastes; those who could afford to live in the newer housing along the terrace, that is.

The house was spacious and had three floors to it. The servants, a house maid, a cook and a scullery maid, had the highest level, and the family the lower two. Mrs Pennington hoped that when they could afford a carriage they would have a liveried groom and stable lad, but her sea-loving husband had no interest in such a waste of his money. It was one battle Laura doubted that even her mother could win. But the empty stall that had been used as a boat house temporarily gave Laura an idea.

She was relieved to see their housemaid and her childhood friend, Annie Biggs, in the hallway. Annie used to play with her as a child when they both lived in the old hamlet, before Mr Pennington had become rich. They were inseparable, always said they would stick together like sisters through thick and thin, but then their lives changed and their paths were no longer parallel. Back then, Laura's father had only a small fishing boat, a coble, that had been passed down to him by his father, just like all the other fishermen, but he had one thing they did not: the ability to see an opportunity when it crossed his path.

Laura looked around her at the new, almost untouched, home and felt sad. The cottage of her childhood always felt lived in, with neighbours coming and going, but here people only came if they were expected. Her mother had also changed. Admittedly she had never been one to laugh or sing. However, she had become increasingly dour and removed from the people who had once been her friends and neighbours. She read about what was expected of a lady, learnt how to run a 'proper' house, and had now absorbed herself in the problems associated with raising a daughter fit to be 'brought out' in society and found a suitable husband.

Annie's father, however, still toiled hard as a fisherman in the small village below on the sandy shore, nestled under the ancient three-hundred-foot-high headland of Stangcliffe, but now the boat was not his anymore; it was rented from Pennington, just as his cottage was.

"Where's Father, Annie?" Laura whispered, glancing in the morning room as she passed by.

"I think he is in the coble, off to look at the new boat down in Whitby. He said that he won't be back till late and to leave him a cold platter for his suppertime." She must have seen the distress on Laura's face, so added, "Your mother is in there, reading." She gestured to the open doorway.

Laura was very disappointed. She had so wanted to seek her father's help and advice. He kept himself busy, but Laura felt there was more to it than sheer demand. It was as if he would keep away from the house, or his wife, as often as he could. Her mother was difficult, Laura knew that, but he was her husband and so should be there for her, at least some of the time. It worried her that if life continued this way they would soon live completely separate lives. When he did return, Mrs Pennington often had a list of things to tell him he had neglected to do and plans for social gatherings that he was ill-equipped to attend. But her father was a charismatic man and on the few times he had attended a formal event his bravado and confidence had either won the people over or at the very least amused them and given them something to talk about. Laura wondered if this was how Daniel Tranton had come to know of him.

"Biggs, is that you?" Mrs Pennington's voice echoed around the hall.

"Yes, ma'am," Annie answered.

Laura shook her head to tell Annie that she did not want to make her return known. The last person she wanted involved in her latest adventure would be her mother. If she heard about a runaway she would call the militia in and then, having ordered them to do their duty and secure the town, would have taken to her bed with the burden of it all. Mrs Pennington was not a lady to underplay a drama.

"Then stop loitering, girl, and bring me some tea. I have such a thirst on me — no doubt having to shout at you has caused it. Can you not come to me when I ring the bell?"

Annie rolled her eyes at the ceiling before walking calmly into the room; she dipped a little curtsey to the rather large figure of Mrs Pennington.

"I'll bring your tea shortly, ma'am. I did not hear the bell. Perhaps it needs fixing again," Annie answered politely, but in a very direct tone.

"Good heavens! Do you seek to tell me what needs doing now? And you a flibbertigibbet of a lass, no older than my own daughter! Where were you? Not wasting your time and our money dallying by the beach, I hope. Now that I mention her, where is my daughter? I have not seen her today." She held both her hands tightly on her lap and glared at Annie.

"She went out earlier on an errand this morning, I believe," Annie lied.

"I will speak to Mr Pennington about this. She is not his errand boy. The man has no idea how hard it is to find that girl a suitor. Goodness, is our only child to be left here, an old maid? She would have the hands and manners of a common fisherwoman if it was left to him!"

Laura was looking through the door jam and cringed at her mother's words. She noticed Annie's hand form a ball as she listened, even though her face remained impassive, for her mother, Ivy, was a fisherwoman and had a good heart. It was not that many years ago that she had been welcome in their cottage.

"Who will look after her when I go to heaven?" Laura's mother dabbed a lace handkerchief to her forehead and sniffed. "For I will one day, and that selfish girl never stops to think of the time when I will not be here. Instead, she ignores me. I will need a companion soon, as I have not had her company for so long." She let out a sigh of self-pity.

"Yes, ma'am, but she is an early riser and I think she finds many things to occupy herself with." Annie stepped back a little as Mrs Pennington's face changed from self-pity to anger.

"You are not paid to think, girl, and if I seek your opinion then I shall ask it. You girls have no respect for the wisdom of your parents. We look to the future, whilst you wallow in your present. She must marry! Her cousin will inherit all our wealth if she does not and then our work will be for nothing. That's who'll take over my home from us if anything happens to Mr Pennington, Mr Reginald Blagdon and his insufferable wife, Amelia; she is an uncharitable woman if ever I have known one and I suspect has French blood running in her fickle veins ... and he, a mere tanner!" The heated tone of her voice subsided as she must have realised her thoughts had run off too fast with her tongue. "Biggs, get me that tea and stop wasting my time!"

"Yes, ma'am," Annie said, and left the room, closing the door quietly behind her. She looked at Laura who had moved away, trying to cover her shock at the content of her mother's outburst.

"Well, I for one was not expecting that. Am I an old maid, too? Do I have the hands and manners of a common fisherwoman? I am not meant to think — well, that's news to me. I'm glad she allows me to breathe, but then I'd have difficulty fetching and carrying for her if I didn't, so she'd care about that!" Annie's cheeks were high in colour.

Laura bit her lip. This was awkward. As her friend she felt sorry for the girl's hurt but she knew Annie should not speak that way to her, especially about her own mother. Her position was one that should mean she kept her thoughts to herself. Laura had not the heart to rebuke her, though.

Laura shook her head. "Mama talks out of frustration. She is lonely and has too much time to think. Please be tolerant of her. Mama is only trying to find her place in life; the house is new as is her way of living. She will settle to it, you'll see. You are happy working here, aren't you?" She smiled but her heart knew that the truth was the girl hated it. Hated her mother and she could not blame her, for she too missed the mother she knew as a child, as she had changed into such a snob, the very kind of person they always despised.

Annie looked at her and then at the new shoes she had been given as part of her uniform. "I do not mean to appear ungrateful. You know I need this job; it makes life easier for mother as she has worked so hard for so long. Her hands do need a rest now or they will be unable to do simple tasks. The cold makes her knuckles sore and her hands become swollen. It's just your mother takes on so and puts me down in such a high-handed way and never asks after mine. They used to share time together, eating and drinking as friends. Now it is as if my ma is dead to yours and that hurts her. She is always asking after Gladys — what am I to say? Then, well, I thought Sid and me had an understanding and yet he went off with Alice — why?" She sniffed and wiped her eyes on the back of her sleeve. "We kissed, Laura. I thought that meant that we were walking out properly. I feel dirty and he knows that I love him so. Why has all this happened to us? Are we not as good as your family?"

Laura took Annie's arm gently by the elbow and led her along the hall to the servants' stairwell. "Of course you are. No one could doubt it, it is just that Father had ideas and they paid off, but he pays your pa well. He's a good man."

"Aye, he is that." Annie sniffed, and her eyes were downcast and did not meet Laura's.

"Annie, was that all you did? Just an innocent kiss, I mean?" Laura asked, thinking it was quite enough really.

"Yes! What do you think of me? I should never have said anything. I'm not a dollymop! Do you look for gossip to spread around your newfound friends?"

Laura looked at her. "What friends?" Then she added, "You're not a what?"

"I am not a fallen woman if that is what you think of me." Annie looked at her as if she should know what it meant.

"No, I don't. Of course not, I meant if the beast had pressed you to … well you know, then he should be…" Laura was rapidly sinking out of her depth and time was passing. "I know you have a good character but sometimes men take advantage of that... Don't they?" She tried to sound knowledgeable about something she knew not.

Annie stepped toward the stairs. "Oh, Laura, you have much to learn in life. You are sheltered from it all up here. Read your books, see what they can teach you about real life."

Laura almost panicked, realising that she had become sidetracked from her task and thought of Daniel waiting for her. His deep blue eyes would be cross, she thought, and pondered what a lovely colour they were — like rich sapphires. Then realising she had drifted again, she suddenly announced, "I need two warm blankets, strips of clean cloth, salve and bread, ham, ale or milk. I will go and find a lamp. Please be quick and discreet, Annie." Laura thought that the note of authority in her voice would work, but it did not.

Annie did not move. "What are you about, Miss Laura Pennington?"

Laura did not care for the sarcastic tone in Annie's voice. "That is none of your concern, Biggs." Laura tried to sound firm in her lowered voice.

However, Annie, who had now fully recovered from her upset, looked straight back at her with a determined stance that told Laura she was not going to do as she was ordered without further explanation. She raised one eyebrow. "I've just remembered I have to see to the mistress's tea so I've no time to stand here gossiping. Sorry, I can't help, I must serve my mistress first."

Laura swore to herself in frustration.

"Annie, please, I…"

Annie sighed. "I have already told a lie for you once today, Laura. If you are hiding something, and you want my help to take things from this house, then you had better tell me why, because my position is at risk if I am found out, whereas you would get away with an ear bashing..."

Laura nodded. "There is a hurt boy who needs my help, just for a few hours. Please, I must hurry, and thank you for covering for me with Mother."

Annie smiled. " I will have to sort Mrs Pennington out first, but if you wait for me by the yard door I will bring the bundle there. But, Laura, you take care. I heard gunshots earlier and there is no gamekeeper on the estate today. I'd know because Abel is a beater when he hunts and he has gone with the master of the big house over to Gorebeck moor. I hope your help does not involve anyone bad?"

It was because Annie was a friend and needed her job that Laura did not illuminate her any further; besides, if Annie confided in her mother the whole of Ebton would know that Jeb was being hidden by the Pennington's. The entire thing was a mess and she wished that she had never laid eyes on the handsome face of Mr Daniel Tranton.

Half an hour later, Laura walked around the back of the tall buildings as casually as she could and tried to keep a genteel, even gait so that she did not appear rushed to anyone taking the air along the top promenade. The moment she slipped into the alleyway between the terraces she quickened her step and put the hood of her cloak up to cover her head.

Laura was delighted to find Annie was waiting for her on the back step. Her friend was smiling at her, though, as if she was very amused by something.

"What are you so happy about, Annie?" Laura asked, glancing behind her, but there was no one else there.

"You, Miss Laura, why are you wrapped up so warm when the day is so bright and sunny?"

"I do not wish to be noticed!" Laura explained, realising that perhaps she was not as good at being clandestine as she had thought herself to be.

"Laura," Annie softened her voice, "you will stand out whether you use a cloak to hide the bundle or boldly march it along the promenade carrying it. You are not a maidservant, so whatever would folk think of you carrying such a burden?" Annie raised her eyebrows, obviously finding the whole situation amusing.

"Well, I have no choice. Someone needs my help and I have given my word that I will not abandon them..." Laura bit her lip as if to prevent any further information slipping out from between them. "I aim to keep my word," she said and dismissed the image of her father's irate face again.

"Find the doctor or take him down to the village; they'd help a lad in trouble. I do not know what you have got yourself involved with, Laura, or why, but I do not want either of us to end up in trouble, do I? Where are you going with them things?" Annie prodded the bundle.

Laura edged slightly; how much was safe to say to her? She had no time to think upon it. "I need to slip unnoticed into the woods..." Laura looked down the backstreet, which was thankfully empty "It is better for you that you do not ask me anymore. Trust me, it is just a temporary problem, no need to involve Mother."

"Well, I wasn't going to rush and tell her your woes, was I? Trust goes both ways, Laura, don't forget that... You go to the gardens behind the old village and I will meet you by the woodland at the back. But, Laura, this will cost you a new ribbon if all goes well, and if I end up in bother, you will have to see me right," Annie said and held firm to the bundle.

"Very well," Laura agreed and walked at a casual pace in the direction of the steep bank that led down to the old village, her cloak billowing noticeably behind her as she made her way down.

Annie took the bundle quickly along the ancient path that was considered too steep for the gentle folk to use and met Laura by the edge of the woodlands.

"Thank you for doing this; I will have words with Mother about seeing yours." Laura smiled, genuinely grateful.

"Aye, well if you can put that right then I'll believe that them pigs on Samuel Driften's farm really can fly. Take care, Laura, you're no good at this kind of thing — you're too honest." Annie winked at her.

"I will — you underestimate me, Annie." She turned away before Annie could say more.

Laura disappeared quickly into the cover of the trees, holding the bundle firmly under her arm beneath the cloak, and making her way as quickly as she could back to Daniel Tranton and the boy, Jeb.

"Thank goodness you have returned! I had begun to wonder if you had become too scared to help." Daniel Tranton took the things from her and had the lamp lit in a moment.

"Such faith you have in me!" Laura said but was ignored. "When I give my word I keep it. I told you, I am not scared of any man." Laura spoke with conviction and he nodded this time instead of offering a rebuke.

"Then I hope you never have cause to be. I see that you saw the wisdom of not bothering your father. That is just as well as I do not want his reputation sullied in any way. I admire Obadiah for achieving all he has in life. Besides, there is a matter between us, your father and me, that is not as clear as I thought it should be." He paused; his expression curious. "Are you aware of it?" "Am I aware of what?" Laura asked, wondering why he spoke in riddles and did not just come out and say openly what he was referring to.

He studied her for a moment as if he was expecting her to say more.

"Please speak your mind. I do not like puzzles." Laura felt vexed with him. He seemed to be taking control of her life in some strange way, making claims upon her time and sanity, spoiling her already threatened freedom.

"Very well, we shall leave that for now. But tell me this: have you seen me before, in Gorebeck perhaps?" he asked.

"No, I had never set eyes on you before you grabbed me so boldly." She stared at him, trying to rack her memory but she had no recollection of his face. Why ever should she if his business was with her father? He made no sense at all.

"Have you heard of me, perhaps, at the assembly rooms?" he pressed.

Was the man so vain that he thought word of him had spread throughout the region? Laura was amazed at his self-obsession. Did he really think that every young maid in the district knew of him? "No! Why should I?" Laura replied. "Are you infamous?"

He ignored her sarcasm.

"Then you know of no letter or arrangement?" He stood before her, staring down as if he was trying to fathom something within her words.

For a moment Laura was transfixed as he held her gaze, as if it was she who was playing a game with him, yet he was blatantly toying with her. "I only know that for a man who has so much pressure on his time, you seem to have plenty of it to ask nonsensical questions."

Jeb coughed.

"Very well. As I said, I would not want to damage your father's reputation." Daniel looked at Jeb, but his mind seemed elsewhere.

"But mine does not matter?" she queried. If he could take time to find out if his reputation, whatever it was, had travelled as far as the coast then she could take the time to knock it down. Laura also had a reputation and family name to uphold.

Jeb coughed again.

"Yours? Well, not to sound indelicate, Miss Pennington, but you had already played dangerous games with your own reputation by trespassing on another man's land, unaccompanied, and getting yourself nearly shot in the process. You are fortunate it was me who found you pinned to the bank; your skirts pulled awry. Otherwise, more than your reputation could have been lost to you. Then no man would even look at you as a marital prospect!"

Laura was shocked. This personal attack upon her character was crude in its delivery. "How dare you! You need my help, remember."

"Do you not see that you could have been in a very perilous situation? What lady would crawl around in the dirt like that?" His manner had now changed to one of indignation.

Laura wanted to slap his arrogant face, but she had never before hit anyone, let alone a stranger. Did he seek to ruin her reputation or merely destroy her confidence? Was he going to hold this information against her? Laura could see he cared enough to help Jeb, but not a jot for her. She decided to answer as she felt a lady should. "If you think so little of me then I will bid you good day. You have taken the care of this boy upon yourself; you can see him right. I will trouble you no more."

He took hold of her arm and pulled her nearer to him. "I am not trying to belittle you, Miss Pennington, for it would not be in my interest to do such a thing if your father's offer is in earnest. I am merely trying to make you see the danger you placed yourself in. You are no child, but a beautiful young woman. I merely point out that what you did was ill advised at the very least and you should seek to humour yourself within your lovely new home and be more wary of walking out. You have spirit and are an attractive young woman, but that can be spoilt so easily if you cross the path of a man who is no gentleman, and you tell me who would be the fault of your ruin then!"

Laura was going to retort, but Jeb coughed even more loudly this time, exaggerating his condition, and so she fell silent. Daniel Tranton's words were true. Laura was jolted back to reality as he spoke words that filled her with fear.

"I shall only be a few hours, but if you stay here I will return before dark and will take him to a safer place." He stepped away.

Laura was overcome by a wave of panic and this time it was she who reached out, grabbing hold of his sleeve. She was not sure which of them looked more surprised. Instantly she let go of it.

"Please, I must be home soon." Laura looked at those eyes and knew that she would do as he bid her, as there was a young life in the balance. How she would explain to her mother where she had been, goodness only knew.

"Stay with Jeb, please." He placed a hand on her shoulder and this time she did not pull away from him. Her attention was his. "They have put a price on him, so do not trust the villagers and ask for help. They would turn the stranger in without it pricking their consciences."

"They are kind people," Laura added defensively.

He smiled at her. "Do you see the good in everyone, except perhaps me? They are hardy people who have had a harsh life existing on a rough shore, with a seasonal income and a lot of changes. Do you think they all admire your father? Don't you think some will resent his success on the back of their loss of a less worthy occupation — smuggling?"

"My father is respected and loved." Laura watched as Daniel gently shook his head and removed his hand.

"Laura, stay or go, but you hold a boy's life in your hands and I believe you have a conscience. Take my advice and do not reveal his presence to these villagers. You will be worldlier one day, but for now accept that what I tell you are words meant to save pain and not to upset your strong and admirable sense of loyalty."

Without waiting for a reply he left.

Laura stood transfixed for a moment as she fathomed the depth of his message. Was her father loved or loathed? Had he been seen as someone who was splitting the old town from the new? If so, what else was true that she never realised? Laura stood straight and decided that, as soon as she had dealt with the problem that had been set before her, she would put time aside and have another good chat with Annie.

"You don't have to stay, miss." The feeble voice echoed around the earthen walls of the old smugglers' hide. The evidence of what it was once used for was still there with a small keg left abandoned. Laura pulled it over to where Jeb was laid down, wrapped tightly in the blankets. She unwrapped the cloth around the small jar of salve. Annie had thoughtfully included a small bottle of vinegar and placed an offcut of muslin next to it.

"You have a graze on your arm. I would like to see it and, whilst we have the lamp light, now would be a good time."

The lad inched himself up to a sitting position and gingerly pulled off his rough-cut jacket. He cringed and Laura eased the fabric from his shirt. Then she slipped him out of the dirty shirt that clung to his skin around the cut. Taking the piece of cloth and the vinegar she began cleaning the fabric away and then the cut itself. It was about two inches long and seemed to be a clean wound. Jeb grimaced as the vinegar stung. Once this was done she removed his shirt and could clearly see that he had been bruised also. There were some marks on his back that looked older, as if he had been beaten before with a stick. This convinced her even further that she must help him. Silently she applied the salve to the wound and then wrapped the clean cloth around it to hold it in place.

"If your friend, Mr Tranton, does not return within the next few hours, I will have to leave you for a while, for I will be missed, but I will return under the cover of darkness, and then I will smuggle you into my home." She tried to sound confident, but she was scared for him. When her father returned she would try and talk to him, see if he would help. The consequences would be harsh for her, but not as life-threatening as they would be for Jeb if she did nothing.

Jeb's eyes widened. "Why would you do so much for the likes of me? You is gentry, I'm nothing!" His voice almost broke as he fought with a wave of gratitude.

"I may live well enough now, but there was a time... Never mind, you should never say you are nothing — everyone is someone and worthy of respect. I am only doing my Christian duty and helping you as you are hurt." She tucked the blanket around him.

"Thank you," he said quietly, then added, "Many would not look my way, Christian or not. My fate is my own." He shrugged, tentatively. "You think he is my friend, then?"

Laura was surprised. "Mr Tranton? Don't you? He appears to be going out of his way to help you."

"He is one of the family of them mill owners and they only think of what is good for their wallets. He is Mr Roderick's cousin and owns another mill. Folk say it is better, but that don't mean it's good. All them machines are monsters and the folk that own them are, too. The noise they make could have been borne from the eggs of dragons they are so evil. Then there is the bits of fluff that get in your eyes, hair and on your chest. They make me cough. I want to go to sea. I want to breathe fresh air. I don't want no walls filled with fire-breathing monsters." His mouth set firmly in a line.

"You really are scared of the place, aren't you?" Laura asked and watched the lad nod his head.

"Perhaps he just wanted to take the credit for returning me to them himself. I mean, why not take me back with him if he can get my papers?" Jeb was eased back into his shirt and jacket. "He don't like Mr Bullman, see..."

"Mr Bullman?"

"He is the overseer and he has his men, all ex-soldiers, all brutes the lot of them."

"Was he the one who was shooting at you?" she asked.

"Yes, he was, and his men."

Laura nodded; this man sounded evil.

"I don't think Mr Tranton would want that man to catch me. Then he'd get Mr Roderick's favour for my return and I'd get a beating. But if Mr Tranton has me mended, then he might have someone new that he can use in his own mill who is owing him their life. Either way, he wins, don't he?"

"You have a sharp mind, Jeb, if not cynical for one so young. But why would Mr Tranton risk being shot at, if he was not telling us the truth?" Laura asked. "I cannot believe that he is so short of people to work his mill that he needs to wait for an injured lad to mend."

"Gentry is funny, they have tastes for blood, even risking their own on a bet. No offence, miss." He tried to smile but winced.

"None taken, Jeb. Like I said, I wasn't born to the 'gentry' as you call them. I came from a normal home, my father a fisherman and my mother a fisherman's wife. My father got lucky, that's all." Laura thought for a moment. "Do you think you can walk about a mile with me now that you have eaten?" she asked.

"I'd be recognised."

"Not if you were with me as my maid," Laura answered and smiled.

"Think I'd look too like a man for that," he said, his voice deepening as if to convince her.

"Not if you wear my cloak and follow at my side." She looked at his face in the flickering light and saw a glimmer of a smile cross his lips.

"But your folks, what would they say if they saw me enter your home? The servants would talk. Nah, it is kind, miss, but

I know folk, they wag their tongues and I have a price on me head. Perhaps if you get one of the fishermen to take me on then I could sail away."

"In your condition? I think not. Look, we have a stable built for a horse and carriage, but as yet we do not have one because my father prefers cobles."

"He likes stones?" His face twisted as he clearly did not understand.

"Not cobble-stones, 'cobles', that is what the fishing boats are known as. My father prefers being on the water rather than being jolted along in a carriage."

"I think he'd like me 'cos I do, too."

"We have an unused boat in the empty stable. We can hide you in there. That way I can get you some hot food and you can sleep knowing that nothing will disturb you."

"But Mr Tranton won't know where to find me." He looked slightly panicked by the suggestion. "You think he is my friend, don't you?"

"He knows my family name. He also must think me stupid to believe that he could retrieve his horse, ride an hour to Gorebeck, seek out and make agreement with his cousin and return before darkness. No, we shall be safer moving you to my home."

Jeb looked at her. "I'll go with you. I've never been a maid before."

There was something about the lad's manner that Laura took to. If her father knew Mr Daniel Tranton then he could send word to him. If not, the lad might find a home in one of the fishermen's cottages down coast. If he was so averse to mill life and had no family, he may as well serve a life on the sea. Her main concern was that the lad's arm did not turn bad, although she could see someone had tried to clean it already.

Once the clouds came over and dulled the bright sunlight, Laura declared it was time to leave. She wrapped the cloak around Jeb and arranged the hood to hide his face and rolled up the blankets so that he could carry them under his good arm.

Laura led him up the steep path out of the woods to the west cliff and then to the alley behind the terraces. The only people they passed by were too busy about their daily chores to pay the lady and her maid any attention.

Before light had faded, Jeb was made comfortable in the bottom of the coble, resting on his folded blankets with an oiled cloth over him to keep him warm. He was quite exhausted from the climb, but at least, Laura thought, he was now safe. Then the rain began; she counted her blessings that she was no longer in the woods, for the climb back up with Jeb would have been nigh on impossible in that torrent.

Daniel rode into Gorebeck, which at its eastern side was still a pretty and growing market town. As he crossed the bridge, near the church, he followed the road past the old barracks, now hardly manned, and toward the loop in the river where the mill building loomed high amongst the surrounding trees. He entered the yard and dismounted without stopping to admire the view, handing the reins of his horse to a lad who was crossing the yard to meet him. It would have been Jeb had it not been for recent events.

Daniel knew he had to play his hand carefully with Roderick. He made his way directly to the office where Roderick would be ending his day poring salaciously over his precious ledgers; no doubt answering letters and petitions.

He was for reform and had the benefit of running his own mill, small as it was, it was profitable and had potential, without cruelty. There was a growing sense of distrust nationally, regionally and he was beginning to suspect — locally. London never looked north, that was the key problem, they did not see what was happening and as long as the profit flowed back to its coffers, it did not really care.

Daniel felt guilty for involving the Pennington girl. She was pretty and daring for a young woman, but she had stupidly wandered onto private land and nearly got herself shot. Hamilton was obsessed with protecting his privacy after his own mills had been the target of machine wreckers in their old home. At some considerable expense the man had erected fences and had two ornate gates built that were locked all day. They were opened when the family left in their carriage or visitors were expected. Visitors rarely came. Mrs Hamilton was a grey looking lady who was rarely seen. Hamilton definitely wanted to send out a loud message that anyone who approached them as a stranger was unwelcome. The Hamiltons' had only purchased the estate the summer before; they had arrived from West Yorkshire and were also representative of new money and blood into the region. Their money, like Obadiah's, was earned rather than inherited, but Daniel knew that it had come from some pretty dubious trading through Bristol, before the abolition of slavery.

As he approached Roderick's office the comparison between his cousin and Obadiah Pennington could not have been starker. Obadiah had worked hard for everything he had achieved and understood the people who toiled for him and who he relied upon to keep his various ventures going, whereas Roderick had inherited a business and treated everyone who worked for him as a minion, showing no respect. Except for Bullman and his men, who seemed to have gained an upper hand on Roderick — how and why? The door was ajar and he could hear his cousin tut-tutting and slamming a drawer closed. Daniel knocked on the door frame and Roderick looked up.

"Come in, come in, damn you. Can't you see I'm busy?" he said, acknowledging, reluctantly, Daniel's presence. "Don't stand about like that, you are a gentleman not a common labourer. Slouching is not the trait of a gentleman, but," he sighed, "I must forgive you for how would you know the difference? Stand with a straight back, man! Did you learn nothing at the school your parents paid for?"

"I learnt many things, Roderick. Tell me you are not still sore because your father cut your education short?"

"I learnt more at my father's desk about this business than you and your pampered pets would have done in any of the great public schools. Now, what brings you here? Be quick, because I am a busy man." Roderick regarded himself as a self-made man despite the fact that he had inherited the mill from his father before him. He still held on to the delusion that it was his business acumen that kept the thing going.

Daniel forced half a smile, even though he knew the gesture would not be returned. Looking at the array of papers and petitions on the desk in front of Roderick, he sat down opposite him. He could see why his mood was particularly dark. "Have you heard of the rally the workers are holding next week on Gorebeck Moor?"

Daniel watched the man's beady eyes glare back at him.

"Heard about it! Of course I've heard about it, man. I hear of nothing else. If it's over fifty people gathered then the militia should attack them before they attack us! Even the bloody magistrate has given permission — does he not read the papers? I tried to get that useless bunch of so-called soldiers down at the barracks to stop it, but will they? The rabble will spread their sedition, treason, insurrection and it will lead to open rebellion and they will not stop until they have our heads!" He sighed heavily.

"Roderick, it is just a meeting of local workers. I think you need to keep a clear perspective."

Roderick looked like he was about to explode. "My demands go unheard. Did they not read how to handle them from the reports in the *Times* on the St Peter's Field uprising in Manchester — they stopped them, didn't they? And why do they think to hesitate? Because our foolish government is frightened of a public backlash after that fiasco! It makes a mockery of reading them The Riot Act!"

"This summer has been hot, taxes have been high, rents doubled and the Corn Laws are unjust and need challenging," Daniel stated.

"You are as soft as butter on a summer's day, Daniel! They should have stood their ground and rid the country of the lot of them. We've all gone soft. We fought Bonaparte to stop this sort of thing happening here and they allow it to go ahead! Revolution is coming, you'll see. We will be answerable to the rabble!" He threw the pen down on the desk. "And you no doubt support them in their stupid ideology?" He glanced down at his ink splashed ledger and his face almost crumpled, lips tightly shut and lines formed as he squinted at the mess he had just made.

"Calm yourself, Roderick, your face has turned red." Daniel could see he was not in a mood that would be lenient to the plight of a runaway.

"No wonder my colour is up, it is my blood that's up, it boils and simmers with every petition these rabble rousers send me. Don't push this away lightly, my young cousin, because we are all in this together. You have a mill and you are one of us."

"My mill gives my workers good food, wages, clothes and education," Daniel said proudly. "Some of the manufactories in the west are no better than slavers. It is that bad, Roderick, and we do not want to be associated with that way of thinking, do we?"

"Aye, I can see it clearly. You, cousin, are part of the problem. You pamper them and give them ideas above their God given station in this world. How you fund it, I do not know, as we are in recession and a crisis is looming. We have competition and we have ungrateful wretches who would destroy the very machines that the manufactory relies upon." He paused and wiped his forehead with his kerchief.

"Have you retired Mr Bullman and his cronies at last?" Daniel asked innocently.

"No, I have not. But if I find he has been sitting in an alehouse drinking instead of finding the runner, I will do — you'll see. Don't think I am not capable of dismissing whomever I choose to." Roderick stared blankly at him. "Was there something else? Like I said, I'm a busy man, even if you are not."

"A runner?" Daniel continued.

"Aye, a young lad. Flitch is his name. Stupid boy injures himself one day and runs away the next. You'd think he had a death wish." Roderick sat back in his chair and sighed. "He will be made an example of when I get my hands on him; revolutionaries the lot of them."

Daniel almost pitied his cousin. He was so filled with angst that it looked as though it was eating him away. His pallor was almost grey, his skin lined; Daniel thought he appeared tired and lacklustre.

"Why send Bullman to chase a scrap of a lad? Surely, your men are better used here looking for possible wreckers or troublemakers. They could be playing cat and mouse with a wretch who will be dead in days anyway." Daniel spoke casually, as if he had no great interest in the matter. Then inspiration hit him. "Will you be going to the Hamiltons' ball next month?" Instantly he had Roderick's attention and with it the man's colour returned. "Sarah Hamilton is a fine young woman; she was quite entertaining when last I visited. I think I shall attend."

Roderick's face went a slightly deeper shade of red and Daniel knew that he had hit a nerve. The man almost salivated at the mention of her name, but his eyes bore into Daniel. Old man Hamilton was obsessive about Sarah. He wanted to net her a good catch, a husband of either rank or wealth, but one that would certainly advance his own ambitions.

"Yes, I am. Why? You're surely not going, are you? You should leave the girl alone; you have no intention of marrying yet." Roderick scowled. "You'll be bored there. Hamilton is a man who does not suffer fools gladly. Besides, he only invites a few acquaintances who he trusts and who are of good standing and keen intellect — so you would definitely be misplaced."

Daniel waited a moment before answering. He could have retorted, insulted Roderick in turn, put the man in his place but he wanted him to sweat. Daniel wanted Roderick to feel that his personal ambitions were under threat. Seeing Roderick's anxiety grow, Daniel acknowledged to himself that he was enjoying playing his hand. Sarah was quite pretty, delicate in looks and disposition. She was younger than Daniel by a year and Roderick by five. His cousin had an interest in her, but Daniel knew he was more handsome and Roderick feared that she had an eye for him.

"That was 'if' I went…" Daniel said.

"I tell you, you will be wasting your time," Roderick persisted, a bead of sweat appearing on his brow.

"I might be, or I could be persuaded against going." Daniel answered.

Roderick let out another sigh and leaned back in his chair, obviously realising he was about to be coerced in some way. "Damn you, Daniel. You come here to taunt me. Is that the reason for your unannounced arrival? You have not come about any damned meeting but to make a play for my intended — for she will be, I assure you. I play cards with her father so don't go giving her any stupid ideas in your direction." He leaned forward and pointed at Daniel. "What do you want?"

"Close the mill for a day and let your workers attend the rally. Show that we are united in our commitment to take their requests seriously…" Daniel's words flowed quickly, hoping to catch Roderick off-guard.

"Demands!" Roderick snapped. "They make no requests…"

"Well? You asked me what I wanted and now you have it … so?"

There was a pause whilst Roderick thought, but then Mr Bullman burst into the office, cutting across their discussion. Bullman explained that he had no word of the boy and stared back down at Daniel longer than was polite, even for a man of equal station.

Roderick exploded, "You could not catch a fish in a dried upriver bed! Get back to work."

Bullman's expression showed his annoyance at being rebuked. "I've sent the word out that if he is found a reward will be had."

Roderick's face was now the colour of puce. "It will bloody well come out of your pocket, man, if he is found then. I gave you no such instruction to place a reward for his recovery. That is your job! Now get out of my sight!"

Bullman paled slightly at the last statement, then turned and glowered at Daniel as he left.

Roderick shook his head and let out a long low breath. He turned to Daniel. "I'll close it for half a day with no pay for them."

Daniel pondered this. "Half a day and throw in the papers for your runaway. I have a taste for some sport today."

Roderick considered. "Very well, but I want your word that you will decline the Hamiltons' Ball and leave Miss Sarah to me."

"Agreed!" They shook on it and Roderick sent for young Jeb's papers and had him transferred legally into Daniel's care until he was of age to work for pay.

"One more thing, Roderick," Daniel added.

"What?" Roderick was clearly vexed.

"Lose Bullman whilst you still can. He is too comfortable in his shoes and threatens yours." Daniel saw Roderick take in his words, but oddly he did not retort. "Good day," Daniel said and left.

Daniel stepped outside, smiling and happy that he had achieved more than he had expected to. Evening would soon be upon them and Daniel needed to eat, his horse needed to rest, and then he would take the road to the coast and see how his new acquisition was faring — or that was the plan until a crack of thunder clapped and the heavens opened. Daniel turned the collar of his coat up and made for the inn. His new acquisition was going to have to wait, and unfortunately so was Miss Laura Pennington.

Chapter 4

"Laura! Is that you?" Laura had tried to enter the house unheard, but as she passed the drawing room doorway, the shrill voice of her mother shouted her name.

Laura composed herself and smiled before entering the room. This was proving to be a difficult day and yet it had begun so peacefully.

"Yes, Ma, it's me." Laura walked over to the winged chair her mother was sitting in by the warmth of the burning fire. She leaned over to kiss her mother's powdered cheek, but the woman turned her head away.

"Where have you been?" She did not even look at her daughter. Instead her stare burned into the fire.

"I…" Laura began, but as usual her mother's question had been rhetorical.

"You should call me 'Mother'. You are not a common girl anymore but an heiress, and what is that on your shoes? You walked mud onto my Belgian rug, whatever next? I've had it less than a year and you treat it like the earthen floor!"

"Sorry. Ma… Mother. I'll go straight away and change." She turned away toward the door and then casually added her question. "Is Father in his study?"

Laura used the word 'study', but it was in fact his bolt hole. It had a desk that he used when he must, and rows of many fine books lined the walls, not that he ever read any of them, but he had bought them as a job-lot from a house that was taken by a debtor's creditors. What he did use was his bottle of brandy and the crystal glasses that went with the decanter. His favourite chair by the warm fire was placed next to a small table on which lay his knife to do his scrimshaw when he fancied it. This was his link to his past; his father had been a seafaring man who had worked in his youth on the whalers that went out from the ancient port of Whitby to the south. The scrimshaw knife was one of his few things that he had left from his father and he treasured it, enjoying losing himself in the intricate work whenever the opportunity presented itself. Not even Gladys or Laura would dare move it from its place.

"Your father has not yet returned nor sent word to me of his intentions. I am constantly beside myself with worry for the two of you, but you never give a thought for me here, all alone ... endlessly waiting..." Mrs Pennington sniffed and dabbed her nose with her lace handkerchief.

Now was her chance, Laura thought. "But, Mother, you need not be on your own, for only today Annie commented that Ivy was thinking of popping over. She misses your company so much. You two used to enjoy a good natter together, don't you remember? Just think how much you have to tell her now about your lovely new home and things you've bought. You could show her..." Laura saw a bemused expression set on her mother's face. This conversation was not going well, she realised.

"Have you no sense of propriety? Laura, put those dark days behind us. How can I ever forget our temporary misfortune of that time when you 'natter' with your maid and forget yourself so? We live on the lower cliff now. Our neighbours, like ourselves are all successful people. We are no longer to associate with the commoners in the old village, they now work for us. Ivy would never understand and should not even think of 'calling'" She stared at her daughter, disgust filling the air between them It emanated from Laura with equal measure, who could not believe that she had just heard such words coming out of her mother's mouth.

"A friend once, should be a friend always, she has done no wrong. We should share our good fortune…" Laura deliberately softened her voice as she spoke, hoping to reach out to her mother's heart — to touch at the very least her conscience.

"Laura!" her mother snapped. "It is not our 'good fortune' but the result of hard work and a clear mind that has changed our circumstance. We have been blessed with fortune because we have earned it. Now, Annie, that girl, serves us, it would hardly be fitting for me to associate with Ivy. I have looked after my friend by hiring her daughter who leaves much to be desired in her service of me. She forgets herself too often and you encourage her. Besides, her husband, who I may add is more than willing to while away his hours in the inn, works as a fisherman for your father. Do not forget that I knew their ways when we had to share their world, but we were meant for something far better. So do not let misguided loyalty hold you back for they would not even glance at us had the shoe been on the other boot."

"Foot," Laura corrected.

"I know what I meant, girl."

"I will never understand, Mother, how you can so easily detach yourself from your erstwhile friends and then complain of loneliness. I will go to my bedchamber and change," Laura replied.

"You will, and not just your clothes. You will change that vile tongue and fisherwoman attitude. You will respect me, your father, and be grateful of your new and improved position in life and aspire to greater things."

"I am happy as I am." Laura stood her ground. She was in no mood to back down. She had tried to find a reasonable side to her mother but had failed.

"You will cease to answer me back. I will have you sent to somewhere where those rough edges can be smoothed down and then, my girl, you will do your duty and marry, and give your dear father a Pennington heir."

Laura's mouth dropped open. She had not expected that. However, Laura was intelligent enough to realise it was within her mother's power to arrange it unless her father stepped in. Her mother's 'will' seemed more and more to be done these days as her father busied himself away from the house.

"You look like a cod fish. Compose yourself, the sooner you are matched to one of the Trantons the sooner I can sleep sound again, knowing you have not thrown your reputation and your life away. Now go!" She pointed to the door, but Laura froze.

She felt as though she had been slapped in the face. "The Trantons? How many of them are there? Why would you ever consider contacting them?"

"They are men of property and Roderick Tranton is only based in Gorebeck. They are developing the place nicely. I have heard that they will be building a new hotel soon and a faster coach is to be established to take people to Harrogate. We will soon have associates there who we can visit. We may even buy a new property there."

"Roderick Tranton has a cruel reputation." Laura's mind was spinning. She wondered if that was why Daniel Tranton had rambled on about a letter. She was being offered up to him, with no say in the matter. "When were you going to discuss this with me?" Laura saw her mother's face anger, but there was something else. Somewhere in there, there was a seed of conscience for she actually looked away again. So her heart had not completely turned to stone!

"When one of the Trantons wrote back asking for an introduction. Then we would advise you how to present yourself so that an engagement could be announced formally." Her mother was staring again at the flames of the fire.

"Engagement!" Laura's anxiety rose with her voice. "I would never agree to such a union based upon one meeting. Mother, I am your only child — your only daughter and you would treat me so."

"Yes, for your own good. You will thank me once you have your own fine house and children of your own to fill it. You are healthy and there is no reason to suppose that you would not have sons. My mother had six! Once an engagement is official it is very costly and difficult for a gentleman to back out of the agreement. So, by the time your true nature was known to him, it would be too late for him to walk away from the marriage."

Laura left before words burst out of her mouth that would certainly have got her sent away, never to return unless she was forced into a wedding. She ran up the stairs to her room. Something would have to be done, and soon. It had been a strange day and a long one. She had been rescued, coerced and now was the keeper of a lad who was basically an outlaw. Her father had taken off on one of his trips without a word, and all she could do was wait to speak to him of the nonsense that was coming out of her mother's mouth. But then she stopped her thoughts for a moment. Tranton had received a letter — one from her father — so was it genuine, or had her mother actually written it in his place? She worried for her mother's sanity; her mind was starting to play her false. Her sense of reality blurred into this world of fantasy that she had created for herself. Laura must seek out her father and put an end to this nonsense. Who would return first, though: a bemused Mr Daniel Tranton, or her wandering father?

Laura waited for her father to return, but he did not. Word had reached back from the other fishermen that the storm was bad at sea and his boat had not come back up coast from Whitby. Mrs Pennington had taken a turn of nerves as she had decided that all manner of ill fates had befallen her husband and so had dosed on laudanum to help her into her slumber, which resulted in Annie settling her for the night like a baby.

Annie slept in the upper room of the house but did not go to bed till late. Laura was so worried for the boy in the stables that, despite the storm and the thunder, she put on one of her father's oiled greatcoats and his broad brimmed hat and went to see him.

"Jeb!" she said as she entered the stable. The rain pelted the building badly and the thunder rolled above them. Each clap seemed louder and nearer than the one before and then the flashes illuminated the sky like the gods of old were at war. She prayed her father was safely tucked up in bed in Whitby and not out at sea.

The lad's head popped up above the side of the boat.

"Yes, miss, were you scared by the storm?" he asked. His manner was much more relaxed as if being in the vessel, even one on dry land, gave him comfort. Laura was pleased that he seemed perkier.

"I thought you would be. How is the arm?" She was happy to see him raise it freely.

"Sore, but better than it was. Storms don't scare me 'cos I love the feel in the air. It's fresh, not like the air in the mill. Couldn't abide being trapped in that place and they even locked us in of a night — it was like being in a prison. Only I slipped out before they had a chance to close the door. Quick as a flash of lightning I was, it was an opportunity that don't come around often and when them happen you just got to take a risk." He pointed to the sky through the doorway. "This, it's marvellous, isn't it?" He was grinning from ear to ear and Laura could not help but laugh at him. "Have Mr Bullman and his men gone now?" he asked.

"There is no one searching for you that I know of, including your elusive friend, Mr Daniel Tranton." Her mother's words had cut her to the core and her anger had turned upon the man who had deserted an injured lad to the keeping of a young lady, leaving both of them in peril. From the handsome hero she had earlier decided he was, he had now become a selfish mill-owning brute like his infamous cousin. "I brought you some milk and ham." She passed the food over to him.

"Did you know that there was things stashed in here?" Jeb said.

"No, I didn't," she said. Laura was intrigued. She hitched up her skirt and, leaving the heavy coat dripping over the side of the boat, she climbed up the steps and into the vessel. "What things?"

"Here, look, this seat is like a box. You move this top plank bit and underneath there is a space for things."

"I am sure many boats are like that."

"No, they aren't. I knows because, before I ended up in the mill, I was raised by my granddad, and he used to have a model of a boat like this, as he worked on them all through his life. This boat is seaworthy."

"But you didn't know that it was called a coble," Laura said and squinted at him.

"Sorry, miss, I thought it best not to let on. I love boats and that is why I came here. I wanted to be in one. I thought if I acted lost then it would be easier to..."

"Run away again?" she completed his sentence for him.

"Well, perhaps," he admitted.

"You have to stop running at some point in your life, Jeb."

"I've only just begun," he said, around mouthfuls of food.

Laura was surprised. Her father had told her the boat had a leak and needed to be worked on. "So what did you find?" she asked, her curiosity roused.

"A pistol, bullets, some money and paper; a fob watch and some dried biscuits — oh, and a hip flask with what smelt like brandy in it. If this vessel needed fixing, I would say the work has been finished a while ago and it is certainly being prepared ready for a journey."

Laura looked at the paper, which was carefully kept in a wallet; it was a bond for a hundred pounds drawn on a Bank in the city of London.

"Well, Jeb, you have not taken anything from here."

Jeb looked hurt in the flash of light that illuminated the stables from the open door. "I'm not a thief. I would not have shown you them if you were going to accuse me of such things." He struggled with his one good arm to replace the seat.

Laura placed everything back where it had been found and covered them with the lid. "It was not a question, Jeb. I was making a statement. You are an honest person and I respect that. If what you say is true then I may have left you in a place where you may well be discovered." Laura yawned, she felt so tired.

"You go back to bed, miss. The storm will take a while to blow over. No one is going to move this tonight. You rest and tomorrow Mr Tranton will arrive, you'll see. All will be well."

"Of course it will be," Laura agreed, trying to share the confidence of her young friend. She loved his renewed spirit, but somehow did not share his optimism.

Chapter 5

The rain stopped sometime in the early hours, but the roads leading to the coast were a quagmire. Daniel decided it would be unwise to risk the journey until he was certain the storm had passed by. News of another nature had been brought to him: the peaceful meeting, which was to be held on Gorebeck Moor to address the workers' concerns was to be usurped by West Yorkshire rebels. These were hard men who preferred rebellious action to talk. They tended to break the machines in revolt against the government. If this message was to be believed, then Daniel knew the workers would never have any reform granted to them. If they did not die at the rally that is... If the soldiers were sent in, men would be placed in gaol and the mills would be fixed and run as before, but with bitter distrust on both sides, until all hell broke loose again. He was for the reformers, not the rioters. Striking did not help the poor, they just became poorer. Somehow, he had to stop the troublemakers before they whipped the crowd up into a frenzy where anything they did would be ill thought out and counterproductive.

The boy, Jeb, would have to wait. He decided to send a letter to Miss Laura making it clear that he wanted her to keep the lad safe, and letting her know the boy was now his apprentice and no longer a 'runner'. Daniel would offer recompense to her father for the lad's keep, as he was sure that Obadiah would take him in.

Obadiah entered the Pennington Hotel through the kitchen doorway at the back of the large terrace house as he was in his working clothes. He wiped the sand from his boots on the threshold as a matter of habit but stopped as he saw Mrs King talking to a young boy. The lad had an injury that she was overseeing the treatment of.

"Who's this?" he asked.

"This is Jebediah Flitch who needed help, Obadiah. Some bad men were chasing him and he was hurt. Apparently they were shooting at him on the Hamiltons' estate."

"And what were you doing on private land? Lad, tell me the truth, where are you running from?" Obadiah's large frame towered over a cowering Jeb. Mrs King touched his arm and had him step back.

"I ran from the mill, mister. They scare me to death them machines. I like the sea."

Obadiah sighed.

"Let him stay here, Mr Pennington, please?" Mrs King said.

"Very well, Mrs King, you can keep him here and have that gash tended. If no one comes looking for him then I'll set him to work for us. But if they do, I'll not break the law and have my business damaged. So know this lad: steal and I'll sort thee out myself. Be good and I'll watch your back. But you do everything that Mrs King tells you." Obadiah was waving his right index finger at the lad whose eyes were transfixed by it as he nodded back.

"Yes, sir, I am not a thief, honest, I just don't like being trapped in them machines and I'm getting too big for crawling under them."

"I'll be back later, Mrs King," Obadiah said and winked at her discreetly, before walking back out.

Laura had been up very early despite her late night. She had watched the sun rise, dressed and then made her way carefully downstairs. She crept down the servants' corridor and waited for Cook, whose day always began at first light. Cook went down to the stone corridor that separated the dairy from the cold store and then slipped into the dairy carrying her jug. Laura ran straight out across the yard and into the stables. Then she stopped. She nearly skidded on the wet cobbles as she approached the stable doors, seeing that they were open wide; she walked tentatively inside and strode around the empty space as if she could not believe that the coble had gone, certain that it could not be so.

She stared at the ground and saw the marks of two wheels and then she noticed a couple of hoof marks where mud had settled on the flagstone floor. The boat had been moved and with it Jeb had been pulled out of his safe haven. She had heard no cries for help, but she thought of the items hidden in the boat and felt fearful of what may have happened to Jeb.

Laura ran back inside the house. This time she was seen by an astonished Cook.

"Whatever are you doing here at this time of day, miss?" She looked around. "Has something happened to Mr or Mrs Pennington?"

"Cook, someone has stolen Father's boat!" Laura exclaimed.

"No one has stolen anything. Calm yourself. Goodness, I told them to be as quiet as they could and I thought they had been, so that no one was disturbed. After the rain, the going was soft so it was a good time to move it down the back alley and away. What's a boat doing up on a cliff anyways?" She shook her head and carried on about her business.

"Does Father know? Has he returned?' Laura asked. She followed Cook back inside the kitchen.

Cook gave her a strange look. "Your mother told Annie to get her father to take the boat down to the beach and put it next to your father's other ones by the inn. She said it had no place there as she had a man coming to look at the coach house, as she refers to the stable, miss. The man who is arriving tomorrow sells coaches. She wrote to them a month since and apparently has been awaiting the day with anticipation."

"But when did they come? Why do it in the night?"

"Not night — early. Fishermen get up early, like your father does."

"If he comes back, please find me urgently. I must talk to him."

"Miss, it is their argument, leave it to them... I mean I would suggest you do..." Cook shrugged as Laura spun around without comment and walked through to the hallway.

Laura hurriedly took down her coat from the hallstand and pulled it on. Grabbing her hat, she went out of the house and made straight for the old town, but as she stood at the top of the winding bank and looked towards the gill she saw that it too had suffered in the storm. The shoreline was a mass of broken-up vegetation and soil. The heavy rains had caused the beck to flood. She swallowed.

"Thank God, I did not stay in the small smuggler's cave with him. We could have been drowned!" she muttered to herself, but once again her thoughts were interrupted as she looked to the shoreline. Two fishermen were pushing a boat out to sea, fighting against the breaking waves. Laura peered and squinted, she could just make out another four figures seated inside it, but she could not tell if that was the boat from the stables or if Jeb was still in it.

Laura wished that she could go running down to the old village, just as she used to, welcoming people that she had grown up amongst. However, Jeb seemed to be a quick-thinking lad, he knew his way back to her if he needed help. The thought that the lad was one of the world's survivors gave her comfort, so she wandered along the top of the lower cliff enjoying the view and telling herself not to panic. After all, she was not supposed to know the boat held secrets and hadn't the lad, Jeb, professed a want to go out to sea?

Opposite, further along the row of high terraced houses, a door opened. It was the front door to Pennington's Hotel, another source of her father's pride and joy. Mrs King, the housekeeper there, must have an early riser leaving the establishment, Laura thought. Her heart skipped a beat. The man's frame was unmistakable. Obadiah Pennington was strong — as the proverbial oxen — grizzled of face and weather worn from years at sea, his back straight as a mast. Laura watched as her father stepped out of the hotel. He had not been out in the storm then, or taken refuge in the bay towns between Whitby and Ebton, for why would he spend a night in his hotel and not return home to them — his family? Or if he had just returned then should he not be going to his wife first?

Obadiah looked around quickly and Laura shrank back into the shadows. He then quickly leaned in to give Mrs Myrtle King a kiss, full on her lips. Not a polite peck, although that would have been bad enough, but a full and lingering kiss. Then they parted and he quickly spirited himself away, walking briskly back to the door of his own home.

Laura leaned against the tree and stilled herself whilst her heart, slowly but surely, began to break. She had worried for his life but he had not been at sea in the storm. He had been a few doors away and apparently cavorting with Mrs Myrtle King! Her father ... her lovely hardworking, honourable father was engaging in immoral behaviour with another woman. How long had this been going on? The words repeated over and over in her mind until she thought her head would explode with the stark reality she was now facing: her father was an adulterer!

Laura could cry, she could scream and she could accuse her father of being totally selfish, but all she really wanted to do was to run to him and ask him to explain why. Like a child, she did not want this to be true, but Laura realised that it was so. In all her life she had never seen her father kiss her mother in such an intimate way or indeed seen her mother respond like that, as if she would melt into him. Even from her vantage point she could plainly see there was a strong bond between them.

Laura flinched as another truth hit her hard. The contrast between the warmth of the Mrs King and the distance of her mother's reprimands and complaints was stark. What was there for him to come home to other than a cold and indifferent wife and a self-absorbed, wandering daughter?

She was shaking inside, yet on the outside she appeared as a sea of calm. Laura slowly walked along the path. Would she end up like him? She breathed deeply, grateful for the bracing fresh air and headed home. He had always been straight with her and she had never feared him, but as she entered this house, this place he had created, which had never felt like her home, she cringed. Yet, she realised that now was a time to talk and not to shout, for she had to help him out of this mess that he had created. He was also about to discover that his wife had taken matters into her own hands and moved his precious boat — and unwittingly, with it a lad and, she presumed, her father's private stash of valuables. But why on earth would he hide so much in a boat; surely he did not plan to run away with Mrs King in a coble? He could hardly elope, as he was married already.

Laura saw him entering his study as she slipped inside the hallway. Leaving her hat and coat on the polished walnut hallstand she headed straight into the room after him. There he calmly sat, relaxed in his own private space, the man she had admired throughout her life, loved and looked up to, casually pouring his glass of brandy and placing it on the table next to his precious scrimshaw knife.

He looked up at the doorway as she entered. "Close the door after you, Laura, and keep the warmth of the fire inside the room with us. It is very fresh out there after the storm." He glanced at her thoughtfully as she did his bidding. "You rise before the sun has had a chance to even warm the air."

She swallowed and stared at him, wondering how he could be acting so calmly. Was he not riddled with guilt? Laura stood before him, looking down at his tired eyes, for the first time she saw a lesser man and not the giant that in her head she had to please; hoping in her heart that he would say something before she had to confront him with her own words. She paused.

"You have something on your mind, Laura?" His words, softly spoken, were challenging her to say her piece.

"Yes," she said and although she did not know how, Laura sensed that he knew already what was to come, "I saw you," she said. "Just now, out there… I saw you."

"Good! You often do. Because you should realise that when you step out of this house, you, milady, are on view, too. And I saw you, boldly walking onto Hamiltons' land yesterday after I forbade it." He stared at her, but she did not avert her eyes.

"You dared to ignore my ban. You gave me your word and you broke it!" He looked away, shaking his head, then downed his brandy in one.

Laura ignored any inner pang of conscience; he was in no position to give anyone a lecture on morality and especially breaking of one's word. "That's as maybe, and for breaking my word I am truly sorry. However, Father, do you understand what I am telling you? I saw you!" Her voice rose slightly, partly to offset the acknowledgement that her own slight wrongdoing could reflect she was of similar character to him, but mainly because she could not believe he would carry on with the King woman, not two doors from their home. How convenient — how totally and utterly shameful! She had always believed him to be a man of high standards. For the first time she had serious cause to doubt it.

"When in particular did you see me?" His face turned toward hers as his eyes fixed upon her own; they were not warm like they normally were. Something had changed, in him — in her. Laura fought the urge to allow a sob to escape. Were they never to laugh and hug and go exploring again? Was this the end of their relationship too, as it would inevitably be of his marriage?

"Just now, Father, out there, I saw you... I saw you kiss Mrs King!" Her voice had quietened again and Laura was struggling to keep it from breaking completely.

"So you did, did you? And what would you be doing up and out on the street at this hour of the day — and on your own?" There was no sign of remorse or shock in his voice.

Undeterred, she was determined not to let him off by diverting blame onto her. "I was looking at your boat going out on the waves and trying to see if you had returned to us safely after the storm. Then you came out of the hotel and you … kissed her, blatantly, for all to see."

He refilled his glass and stared at the brandy, swirling it slowly, rhythmically around and around. "What have I told you, Laura, about straying out on your own? You are a young woman of means now. You can no longer wander off at will. Your mother has no control over you and you show no desire to obey my word. What are we to do with you?" He was completely dismissing her words.

"Father! Do not ignore me. I know you are having an af… a liaison with that woman. How could you?" She did not know if she wanted to hit or hug the man. She felt like she was losing him … had lost him, or worse, never had him, not the father she thought she knew. If she felt so betrayed how much more so would her mother be? There was a distance between them that had never been there before.

"Very easily, she is an attractive woman with a kind heart." Laura took a step back. His words were like a slap. He raised his eyebrow and continued. "Do you think your mother cares? Do you think I care if she knows or not? She has what she wants here, her house, her 'palace' to play the part of a queen in, and I have what I want: a warm-blooded woman who welcomes me and who smiles and laughs at my quips. And, Laura, my dear, I will not give her up for anyone, not even you. But, my girl, for your own good you will be leaving us for a while and attending a school in Gorebeck, where a governess will give you instruction on how to act like a proper lady before it is too late. For in the next year you will be married and your errant ways will change. A husband will not allow your wilful spirit and I will not be able to come to your aid if you cross him, but marry, my dear, you will, for your own sake as much as ours." He breathed deeply and then gulped down his next brandy. Morning had hardly broken and his cheeks were already red from imbibing liquor.

"I am too old for a governess to tutor me, and how can you think that mother does not care about such a thing as you have done, betraying her like that. If I saw you, our neighbours could and the scandal would be terrible." Laura was trying not to sob at the reality of the words of his threat.

"Laura, it is my hotel and I have every right to go there when I wish to visit. I was careless this morning, but she had been afeared that I had perished in the storm and I wanted to let her know that all was well... She cares deeply for me." He had the gall to smile affectionately as he thought of his lover. Not a glimmer of a thought for his family, though, it appeared.

"I was worried, Mother was worried, so why did you not come to comfort us first? Don't we mean anything to you anymore?" Laura was practically pleading with him.

"Your mother would be asleep and you, my dear, you disrespect my commands and my wishes. Therefore, I went to one who would not ever disobey me and who I have every faith in. I have made a decision to find a man who you will listen to, who is better placed to safeguard your future. I will seek one out. Now leave me and think on what I have said. You go to the Abbey School next week for two months of intense instruction and you will follow it to the letter."

"If I refuse?" she snapped back at him. She had never openly stood in defiance of his orders before.

"You will be homeless by nightfall." His face was set, lips clenched together in a line. He would do it; she knew it. Even if it broke part of his fickle heart, he would not back down, his pride was too great for that.

Laura wanted to strike out at him. She did not like the way he had so selfishly dismissed her.

"Father," she said and stepped towards him but he raised his hand and prevented her from coming close.

Laura felt a pain, the sheer destructive hurt of rejection. As she looked into his eyes she saw the harsh truth: their relationship had ended — or changed irreparably. She was no longer his 'Little Laura', she had grown up and crossed a line. So how could she strike back? Then a moment of realisation hit her. Her mother had already provided her with the words she needed to hit back at him. "Your boat is no longer in the stable." She saw the annoyance on his face freeze as he heard her words. Laura turned to leave.

"What?" he was standing instantly. "Come back here this minute."

Laura had his complete attention now. It filled her heart with the joy of sweet revenge and even though disloyalty bit at her she pushed it aside.

"I said…" she sighed and saw the exasperations almost ooze out of his skin.

"I heard what you said, but what did you mean by it?" he asked, standing to his full height, his brandy forgotten.

"Just that. The boat that you had stored in Mother's carriage house is no more. Apparently it had been mended already so it is no longer 'stabled' there but is now where it belongs down on the beach. Mother arranged for it to be moved this morning. If you had been here you might well have been able to talk to them when they came and instruct them otherwise if it displeases you. Annie's father, I believe, arranged it for Mother. She said it belonged down with the other boats. Mother has a man coming about purchasing a carriage tomorrow to see what would be suitable, and she wanted the boat out of the way."

"Hell's bells! The stupid woman! Has she lost her senses?" He balled his fists and stormed past her and out of the house, making straight for the line of cobles on the beach. Laura wondered what he had been planning with the bonds and things stashed within it. If her father could cheat on his wife so causally perhaps he was capable of smuggling. She wanted to cry. She wanted to be free of both of her parents for neither of them loved her. They both thought of their own pleasures: one the warmth of a mistress and the other the craving for greater wealth and possessions. She was merely an asset to marry off for further gain to provide a Pennington heir!

If only they had stayed in their simple cottage with their friends and neighbours she would be happy again. But life was not like that. She would escape. But how?

Chapter 6

Daniel set out early to return to his mill. The eight miles were arduous as the roads were heavy going after the storm. He could not help but think about Miss Laura Pennington as he travelled. Whoever married that lady would certainly have an interesting life, or a troubled one. She was a natural beauty, but headstrong, although her tenderness toward Jeb showed that she had a warm heart — definitely her father's daughter. However, her lack of judgement was a concern. Her naivety bordered foolishness in going onto the Hamiltons' estate and leaving herself so vulnerable.

One question niggled at his soul: could he marry such a woman? Would she make him happy for more than a passing fancy? He had expected to marry for love, in his own time, not as an arrangement forced upon him for fiscal reasons. Did he actually want to marry yet? He enjoyed his freedom, running his mill, owning his life now the threat of war had mercifully dispersed. To share his world would mean major changes. At some point he would have to settle down — but he was uncertain if that point was now.

Daniel turned his thoughts to his cousin. Roderick had set his cap at Hamiltons' precious daughter, Sarah, but she was spoilt and frivolous, and would tire of him within the first week of their marital bliss. She would cost him dearly, too — the lady had a taste for fine jewels. Daniel was sure that Hamilton would rebuff Roderick's advances, and if so he would be sure to snap up Miss Pennington quickly. For whatever reason, Obadiah had offered Laura's hand to Daniel first, unless Roderick's letter was still to arrive. If Roderick had received it Daniel was sure that Sarah Hamilton would fade into insignificance, for Pennington had access to invaluable trade routes.

Daniel's mind calculated the chances and prospects of such a match, but what he returned to each time was that he would hate Roderick to get Laura. Why was Obadiah so prepared to wed Laura off without her consent? It was obvious that she knew nothing of her father's intentions. She hardly struck him as a wench who was so biddable that she would follow her father's wishes without discussion.

Daniel stopped momentarily and looked across the moor and down into the vale. First, though, he had his livelihood to protect, not only his, but the whole community that relied upon the mill. Pennington knew the trade routes well. He had contacts going back to a time when his trade was illegal contraband, and Daniel did not want to risk losing them. He wanted to build upon them; for a country that had suffered badly through war was a land of opportunity, and demand for goods would be high. True, he could start talking amongst the other sailors and find new contacts, but that took time and he trusted Obadiah, just as he also trusted him to keep his word and marry Laura off to someone else.

He had been Pennington's first choice — and that was not an honour to be cast aside lightly. If Daniel refused the daughter, there would be no going back, that precious friendship would be lost and his business would be irretrievably damaged whilst Roderick's flourished.

Daniel took the road down to Beckton Mill and was greeted as usual by his foreman, Simon Giles. Smiling, he took Daniel's reins as he stopped the horse by the dismounting block just inside the gates.

"Giles, I have news of difficult times ahead. There will be trouble here if we do not act quickly to pre-empt it."

The smile vanished from Giles' face. He nodded and Daniel instantly knew that all the rumours he had heard were true. Simon Giles was not a man to hold information back from him if encouraged to share it.

"Call a meeting in the yard and bring me a box that I can stand upon. Place it so that they face me with the mill behind me. I want to speak to everyone: man, woman, girl and boy! I want them to focus on what I am saying and the livelihood that will be threatened if they do not support me. Ring the bell when they are assembled and I will come straight out."

"Sir, are you certain you do not wish to discuss it first?" Giles asked.

"No, I know what I have to say. We shall talk later."

An hour later, the bell sounded. Daniel walked out of his office, across the yard and through his workforce, deliberately emerging from the gathered crowd, and stepped proudly upon the box to face them. He was already tall, but he wanted to be clearly seen to stress the message he was about to deliver. If he was to answer to anyone for the industry's treatment of its workers then he would answer to his own people directly, for they toiled long hours to support his lifestyle. If only more mill owners could see this. Instead, they creamed off as much profit as they could and saw the face of revolution in every reasonable request for fairer pay, or shorter hours for their children. Daniel did not. He saw one commonality: they wanted fair terms and he a clean profit.

The look of desperation on the faces over at Gorebeck Mill, the sadness in their eyes and tiredness on their hungry faces had touched him deeply. How bad had Roderick allowed things to get? The people had suffered through the wars with France; they too deserved a happier future. These factors were not so prevalent on the faces he now addressed.

"We cannot afford to stand around here, sir," a solitary voice shouted out, and the noises of agreement revealed the mood of the workers.

Daniel raised both his hands to calm the mutterings and stirring that had begun and then he raised his voice also.

"Hear me out. Your wages will not be deducted for attending this meeting, or for the hour you will be given after it to talk amongst yourselves and decide upon your actions after hearing what I have to say." He saw surprise on most expressions but there was annoyance on a few — he saw plainly who wanted a settlement and who ached for trouble. The newer faces were the ones showing disdain.

There was instant murmuring in the crowd. Curiosity was openly mixed with hostile suspicion. If he judged this correctly he could squash the dissent and appeal to their loyalty, for he had always been fair.

"You have nearly all worked here since childhood. Some of us have even schooled together as nippers."

"Not at boarding school, I bet," shouted a voice, and a low ripple spread amongst them. Daniel continued unabated. "Those of you who remember your first years' toil in the mill before I bought the place out will remember a very different environment to the one you now have the good fortune to work within."

Daniel looked around, deliberately seeking eye contact with individuals that he knew well and was reassured when the older members of his workforce nodded and grunted their agreement.

"I have been hearing some disturbing news recently and I would have my say here — openly before you hear hatred and lies from those who have their own motives for being amongst our people. There is a rally one week from today. A meeting will be held up on Gorebeck Moor to discuss the rights and conditions of all the mill workers, both here and further away in West Yorkshire and Lancashire, but it will focus its hatred here, near our own mill." He pointed to the building behind him. "It is supposed to discuss a fair working wage and the number of hours of employment that may legally be expected for a child to work. It is supposed to address the complaints and issues that workers have with their employers who are not content with their lot. I have been to Westminster and I have spoken to the government on the same issues and supported new bills. However, if you doubt me then listen again. I have already given you my permission to attend, not at your own expense, but on half pay, so half of the expense is mine, when nearby mill owners have threatened sackings for those who attend, or no pay at all for the day. I ask you now to go and talk amongst yourselves and decide if I am being fair to you. If you think not then you are free to take your labour elsewhere for I only want workers who are loyal in my employ. So tell me — am I being fair?"

He had shouted the final question out and was relieved that all immediately nodded that he was being so.

"I have had an open door to my foreman who reports directly to me with any of your complaints, set up here for the past two years, which has resulted in shorter shifts, warm supper in winter and better conditions for you and your children throughout the year. Your food is provided freshly cooked and is grown here on my land. It is shared fairly between the house and the workers. Is this not correct?" Again he bellowed out the question.

"Aye!" was the resounding response.

Once more his heart was filled with pride that these people who he cared for in his own quiet way were responding gratefully for the concessions he had put in place. This had caused more bitter resentment between him and his cousin.

"Therefore, I ask you this — do you still want to go to the meeting? Have you cause to go? And, if you go, when the trouble breaks out because of interlopers from the west, hell bent on breaking our machines, taking away your livelihood as well as mine — will you protect my mill, or let them destroy everything we have worked for together to make our good living?"

He saw the look of realisation on many faces. There were gasps among some of the women, because such stark reality coming from his mouth had brought the truth to them of what their families would face. He noticed the downturned eyes of some of the younger men and knew instantly that his mill had been singled out. But why on earth should it have been?

"I'd protect our mill!" shouted one of his older hands: a loyal man who knew when things were good and would stand by Daniel, for he had lived through the bad times.

"And me… and me…" the voices echoed from men and women and their excited children who repeated the calls of their parents.

Daniel raised a hand to silence them all. "Good, then I ask another question. Is there anyone here who would voice complaint and is still unhappy?" He glanced at the faces who looked less than convinced. Newer faces.

Jerome Sleights stepped forward. "You are a man who stands by his workers and his word, but your cousin is not.

Ivor Bullman and his men run that mill as if it was their own. They make sure no complaint reaches the ears of their master and he accepts that as the good running of his mill. Do you stand with him on this? Will you stand with his workers, too?"

It was a fair question, although there was no link between the mills save for the blood that ran in both men's veins.

"Jerome." Daniel saw the man's eyes widen as he had not expected him to use his name, but Daniel knew the name and family members of everyone there. "I hear what you say and, if you all give me your word you will set up shifts around the clock to protect our mill, then I will return again to my cousin and try to stop him from enforcing any heavy-handed ways of dissuading his workers to attend the meeting. We have survived a bloody, drawn-out war and are now living in difficult times, but we have worked together here to grow our own food. There is opportunity abounding if we work together, but we have to be flexible to get through the lean times. I give you my word that no one will be cast off or starve on my land. But if these outsiders break what we have built up here, the money I will need to invest in new ventures will be taken by the need to mend broken tools. Then the future will not be so bright for any of us and some may be laid off, but I would try to ensure that each family had one working member within it."

Jerome shuffled his feet. "It sounds like a threat wrapped up in promises," he said, but others around him growled disapproval at his disingenuous comments.

"My words are not threats; they are words of truth wrapped up in a vision of the future prosperity that we can all share in. If you have no wish to be a part of it then you are at liberty to leave now and spare these people the distress of having an outsider working against their interests from within our community." Daniel glared at the man.

Jerome looked at the frowns he was getting from his colleagues; the people he had grown up with and worked alongside were now doubting his loyalty.

"You speak the harsh truth of it. I'm a family man and I'm no outsider and any man who accuses me of that again, no matter what their rank, I will ask to stand face to face with me, like a real man, and back their words up."

Daniel stepped down from his box and walked up to the strong figure of Jerome Sleights and stared up at the man who was at least six inches taller than he. "I will stand behind my words and in front of you as a man anytime you care to call me out!" Daniel shouted at him so that every man, woman and child could hear and hoped that he sounded more confident than he felt.

Jerome, who had enough muscles to crush Daniel's skull with one solitary balled fist, smiled back at him. The tense atmosphere dispersed instantly and Daniel felt his clenched innards relax slightly.

"You have my loyalty," Jerome replied. "Now show me your trust. Let me organise the shifts of men to protect the mill, whilst you sort that wretch Ivor Bullman out … sir."

"Come to my office." Daniel turned his back on the man and returned to his box. "You all have until the bell goes in one hour's time to talk over what has been said. If you have no further questions or complaints, return to your duties and no pay will be docked. Then no more is to be said on the matter."

Daniel jumped down, happy that his oratory had gone well and that he had seemingly won over a key man in the factory. Jerome's influence was as strong as his build. The people seeing the large figure of Sleights following Daniel to his office was an image that sent a powerful message to his workers — more than his words perhaps, he reasoned.

"Close the door, Sleights, and explain your meaning," Daniel said as soon as they were inside the room. He may have made generous offers but he was the owner and he commanded respect. He would be fair, but not dictated to or weak. Look what had happened to Roderick with Bullman. "What do you mean by the comments you made about Bullman and my cousin?"

"He oversees your cousin's mill."

"I know what he does, and so?" Daniel wanted to hear what he suspected clarified by another who was better placed than he to discern the truth of the situation. He also wanted clear proof to show his stubborn-headed cousin.

"He makes it known that he dislikes the way you do things here," Jerome continued, but Daniel felt that he was missing something more substantial.

"Be open, man. I will not hold anything you say against you or spread it beyond these walls if you do not wish it known. I will give you my word that on this occasion, even if you incriminate yourself with Bullman in anything untoward, I will not seek punishment for you. I need to know exactly who and what I am up against or we shall all lose out."

"He wants his men to control both mills so that they are run in the same way — his way. If trouble is brought here, then your cousin will blame the liberties you allow us and say they have gone to our heads. Therefore, he will insist on firmer controls being brought in. Of course, he will seek Bullman's advice as to who should oversee the changes."

"It is an interesting accusation, but you overlook one vital point: he has no right to do this, as this is my mill," Daniel explained, "and I would prevent it from happening."

Jerome looked around the room, his arms dropped to his sides and he stretched out his fingers before balling them into fists again. He was ill at ease; he knew far more about what was happening in the region than even Daniel had suspected and that gave Daniel a chill feeling. He looked the man straight in the eye.

"The only way he would gain control of this mill was if something were to happen to me, to remove me in some way," Daniel added, and was taken aback when the man looked him straight back in the eye and ever so slightly nodded but said nothing further. "Are you suggesting that…?" Daniel could hardly believe that if harm was intended for him, his own people would knowingly look the other way.

"I've said too much already, sir, and much of it is speculation because I have no proof. But why would the word I have heard be directed at unsettling this mill rather than the one over Gorebeck way? I've been watching and listening to certain folks for a few weeks and there's been men, strangers, stirring up support for action in the local inns — tarring all your family with the same brush. I saw Wilson, Bullman's right hand man, in the White Hart here in Beckton last week, chipping in his penny's worth, stirring trouble right here in our own village. Why? Unless they want to protect Roderick Tranton's mill?"

"My cousin is not a man who could live with my blood on his hands. Think about the severity of what you imply." Daniel was resigned to the possibility as he spoke, for in his heart he knew that Bullman and his comrades — all ex-soldiers — could come up with any divisive plan to remove him. Yet surely Roderick would not go to such criminal lengths — no, it was too contrived and cold an idea.

"With due respect, sir, your cousin rarely leaves his ledgers to inspect the mill or the inn where he would see Bullman acting like he was lord of the manor. Mr Tranton trusts the running of everything, along with the discipline, to Bullman. His own interests lie in numbers and so long as they add up nicely then he is a happy man — or at least a contented one. He would not suspect how far the man would go. If this mill can make profit, sir, with honest folk who work fewer hours for better pay than Gorebeck's mill, how is it then that their profits are so much less?"

"How would you know if they were making fewer profits?"

Jerome clenched his lips tightly shut.

"You have gone too far already, man, to stop now. You may as well tell me all and I swear I will not reveal who told me anything, but in order to survive I must know the answer to my question or how else shall I protect you all from a tyrant."

"I have been courting a lass from over there, who works in the house and helps in the office occasionally as she has a gift for numbers, and her writing is almost copper plate. He likes his ledgers real neat, does Mr Roderick. She mentioned that the way things were the mill was lucky to be still going. They cover their costs and your cousin's expenses, but not much more. Bullman sells and buys for Mr Roderick, but he takes a cut both ways. Small enough per bale not to be noticed, but over time it makes a good supplement to his wages. This isn't written down, but when she told me how much he said he bought and sold for, I checked with my own cousin who knows the truth of it, for he is a merchant. The man has been lying through his rotten brown teeth." Jerome Sleights words were embittered.

"How long has this being going on?" Daniel asked as he absorbed the stupidity of his cousin.

"A couple of years, as it took Bullman a while to weave his way into a position of trust."

Daniel sighed. "Thank you for your honesty." He thought for a moment. How could he get the proof he needed for his cousin to take his claim seriously? If Sleights was not exaggerating, his own life could be at risk. "Now answer one more question." Daniel took a deep breath before he formed the words he could barely believe he was asking, "Would Bullman go so far as to arrange an attack on the mill as a smokescreen for their main intent, which appears to be to murder me?"

Jerome looked at him square and gave his answer in one word, "Yes."

Laura had gone to her room and remained there for most of the day. She had forgotten to mention Jeb in her heated debate with her father. If the lad had been found then his fate would be sealed. Her father had stormed out of the house like the devil was on his tail. She had never seen him so angry. Apparently he cared more for his boat and the treasures within it than for his own daughter or wife. His soul seemed lost to his sin and he cared not.

Laura needed time to think. There was the elusive figure of Mr Daniel Tranton and the prospect of her father marrying her to him, or at least trying to, she thought, for she had no intention of agreeing. Yet if her father was capable of having a mistress only doors down the row then would he care in the slightest if she wanted to wed or not? Did she really care if her refusal shamed or annoyed him? How many other people knew about his liaison with this woman? She thought about the words of Daniel Tranton. Did he know of Obadiah Pennington's behaviour? The villagers were a close-knit community and, like Annie, watched and no doubt reported back. Oh! Laura held her hand to her mouth. Did Annie know and had not told her but gossiped about him with Ivy? Perhaps that is why Ivy wanted to visit her old friend. Then a thought struck Laura: as her daughter should she tell her mother? Her mind was in a complete whirl.

Hurt was being slowly replaced by anger because she realised this small town that she knew so well was an illusion. Nothing was as it seemed. The fishermen may resent their employer's success as they still toiled for their old friend; especially one who played his family false. She breathed in deeply and then let out a long slow breath to calm her agitation. This could not be borne. Somehow she would find the truth out. Even if her father could, Laura decided that she could not live a lie.

If her father's declaration of love for the widow, Mrs Myrtle King was not enough, she had little time in which to plan or plead her case for she was to be sent away — to a school at her age! Hours had passed and still she had not made a decision on her next course of action. The more pressing the problems felt the less able she was to make a decision.

Looking over the bay through her window she wondered if her father had found his precious boat, or Jeb. When there was a knock on the door she snapped her head around as if woken from a nightmare.

"Who is it?" she asked.

"Annie... I have a tray for you."

"I'm not hungry." Laura wanted her to go away for if there was a hint of gloating in her eyes she would dismiss her on the spot — friend or no.

"There is a letter for you. The man said it was urgent and had to be given to you alone, straight away."

Laura walked over to the door and opened it. "Please leave the tray on the table." For once she had no problem in sounding authoritative.

Annie did so without question but was staring at her. Once it was placed carefully down, she picked up the letter and handed it to Laura. "What's happening ... miss?"

"Did you see the boat being taken away this morning?" Laura asked her whilst she stared at the envelope, her name penned in a strange, but confident hand.

"Pa took it down to the bay with a few of the men as Mrs Pennington ordered, but only waved from the window as I wasn't up and dressed, so I did see them, but not to talk to. Why?" Annie asked.

"Was there anyone there that you did not recognise?"

"No, but why would there be?" Annie was standing next to her, staring at the letter.

"No reason. It all seems a bit strange, the boat being moved without Father's knowledge, that's all." Laura tried to sound dismissive.

"Well, he was ... busy," Annie said, and smiled.

Laura stared at her. "Busy?"

"Are you going to open it, miss?" Annie ignored Laura's comment, which told Laura that at least one other person was well aware of his arrangement. The anger was growing — her father had made fools of them both.

"Yes, I will, after I've eaten." Laura stared at her old friend. Annie was obviously disappointed.

"I thought you weren't hungry," she said, more like her old self.

"Well, I am now." Laura sat by the table and poured out her hot chocolate from the china jug.

"I could help you if there's a problem, L... miss," Annie offered.

"Thank you, I will let you know if there is."

Annie left, for once allowing the door to slam behind her. Instantly, Laura regretted her actions for she could certainly do with a friend at that precise moment and she wondered if her highhandedness had just lost her one. She pushed the tray to one side, untouched.

Laura opened the letter. The writing was neat, but bold, each stroke confidently scribed with a slight flourish. She smiled. It betrayed the man's inner care and precision. So he had an eye for detail. It was, as she expected it would be, from Mr Daniel Tranton, for who else would be sending her mysterious notes? At least her fears that he had abandoned the boy to her care were allayed.

His apologies were heartfelt, or so they seemed. He begged her to ask for her father's help and to look after Jeb until he returned. He had the papers for the boy's apprenticeship, so Jeb was no longer being hunted and was quite safe. Daniel would visit in a week's time, after he had dealt with a pressing matter concerning his mill and the forthcoming worker's rally on Gorebeck Moor. Then the language softened as if he was starting his letter again, in a more personal manner: 'Dear Laura' again — not 'Miss Pennington'. His familiarity touched her, but also she knew how appalled her parents would be at such a forward approach. He continued to tell her that they would be free to pursue more personal matters concerning her father's proposition in the near future.

The last sentence she reread a number of times.

It would appear that fate has thrown us together, so we must see if fate is working in our favour.

Laura stared at it. Fate? Was it true? Could a match between two people be as simply declared as that? Had 'fate' taken over her life? Was she supposed to accept a man blindly because they had a chance meeting? There were so many revelations happening in her life that she could only assume that fate may well have brought them together, but realising what a mess she was now in, 'destiny' could split their relationship apart before it had even a chance to begin. Laura peered out of the window at the open sea; she now wished their relationship could have that chance. She sighed. She had hidden a runaway who was no longer being pursued and had managed to lose him. He had an injured arm, access to a pistol, and money as well as a knowledge of boats. Her mind was reeling; he could set out on a life of crime in order to simply survive, as he had no idea that Daniel had kept his word. Jeb would not be able to handle a boat on his own but could easily stowaway on one.

Laura's father had brought her up as a boy, but with simple wholesome morals. She had gone out in the boats when young, fished and hunted, and on other men's land when needed with his blessing, but now he was a respectable man of business, so she had been ordered to forget the hunger for adventure that ran in her veins. But how? What was she to do — change her very soul, sell it, as he appeared to have done?

She did not want to change, though; she loved her old life, the freedom of the rides in the boats out on an unpredictable sea. Tears overwhelmed her eyes and rolled silently down her cheeks.

Wiping her eyes, she stood up. Who was she trying to fool? Her fond memories were based on lies and deception. Laura decided on action, her wallowing was to end, and her day would begin again. She would seek out her father and ask for his help in finding Jeb; he could hardly lecture her about behaving badly, not now.

By the time Laura had made it down to the shoreline the boat had gone and so, it seemed, had her father with some of the men. A few women sat clustered together, mending nets and gutting fish. Laura saw a woman she knew look up, but she did not respond to Laura's wave. So, she thought, it appeared there was some jealousy in the old town towards her family. How blind she had been. Laura had to continue with her head held high as her father had taught her. She walked up the muddy track alongside the beck that ran beside the gill. It led her to the hiding place to seek Jeb, but her efforts were in vain as there was no trace of him having been there since they left together. With little choice of an alternative action, she made her way back to the lower cliff and headed straight for the hotel — their hotel, although she doubted her father would be back there so soon, but Mrs King may well know what he was about, whilst his wife slumbered on in her laudanum-induced state, no idea how her carefully treasured world was about to fall apart.

Laura took a few moments to straighten her skirts and to breathe in the fresh sea air. Now, more than at any time in her life, she wanted to appear as a woman in her own right. She walked up to the hotel and was about to open the door when it was answered by a maid. She had obviously been seen approaching.

"I wish to see Mrs King," Laura announced. The girl knew her well enough and nodded. Laura entered the hotel, following the maid into the reception room.

"Good morning, Miss Pennington," Mrs King's melodious voice greeted her as she entered. She was a tall woman who had a certain grace about her. Laura hated to admit it, but her father had chosen a pretty mistress, not old enough to have faded looks, but not young enough to be flighty and restless.

"Mrs King…" Laura waited for the maid to leave them. "My father…" Laura began, but realised she did not really know what to say. She just wanted to face this woman who in the previous hours had become a husband-grabbing demon in her distraught mind.

"He is not here," Mrs King answered, pre-empting the question. Her smile was open and warm. Laura felt wrong-footed, she had expected a polite indifference, or a show of subdued resentment, perhaps even shame.

"No, I thought not." Laura stood, looking around her; she had only entered the building once when it was first purchased, then it was plain and empty, but now it had been tastefully decorated. There was something strikingly feminine about it; it felt loved in a way her home was not. The irony struck her hard for this was a hotel, it was supposed to be impersonal, but it was not, yet Laura's home was, as it lacked soul. Her father was somewhat to blame for that as he was never there.

"Miss Pennington, are you not feeling well? Would you like something to drink? Perhaps you could join me in my parlour and we could talk there." Mrs King stood aside and gestured that Laura should walk with her to the back room of the first floor. Laura hesitated but the woman smiled politely and something within Laura responded to her warmth. She had tried to rub as much mud from her boots as she could before entering, but next to this elegant woman she felt like a scullery maid, rather than a lady, the legitimate daughter of the woman's lover. Laura's emotions were spent. From shock, anger, outrage, she now felt that temporary compliance was needed to give her time to think.

This room was obviously Mrs King's own private parlour. It had two chairs placed either side of the hearth, which glowed with growing flickering flames of fire. Each winged chair was covered in pale blue chintz that matched the eyes of the lady who was watching her very closely. It was very feminine and yet on the mantelpiece was the unmistakable pipe of a fisherman. She would know her father's scrimshaw work anywhere. The room was full of his presence. The brandy decanter, the old pair of slippers by the side of the fire tucked away discreetly under a low footstool. My God! Laura thought, this was his home! She felt vulnerable, exposed as her emotions so raw, so shaken, made her swallow and try to stop more tears from pouring out. She was not a child and had done no wrong. This woman was the fallen woman who had destroyed Laura's world.

"Would it help if I said something to you first?" Mrs King offered, gesturing that Laura should sit down and make herself comfortable.

Laura had plenty of things she would like to say to her but words failed her. She nodded. She had come to this place filled with indignation; to confront the woman who had ripped her heart in two, yet instead had been enveloped by a feeling she could not comprehend. It certainly was not hatred. More a sense of loss, of her father, of her security and at a loss as to know what to do next.

Laura snapped her attention back to the woman opposite. A flash of anger freed her tongue as she remembered seeing that kiss — the moment her world froze and shattered. She breathed deeply and spoke. "I saw you this morning, Mrs King."

Mrs King sat before her with a straight back and her hands folded gently on her lap.

"I know you did, Laura. I saw that you were watching your father from across the road when he left me."

Laura looked at her, eyes widening. She could shout as if she was having some kind of tantrum, but the woman was not being apologetic or defensive. Instead she gestured that Laura should sit down, more insistently this time. Laura did so, as she felt in need of support — her legs felt as unsteady as her head was unsure.

Mrs King poured a small brandy and offered it to Laura. Laura was about to decline, but Mrs King seemed to have a second sense. "Take it, miss. Sip it slowly, then let us talk honestly to each other." She smiled but Laura did not.

Laura took it, but before she could speak the lady continued.

"As I was saying, I realised that you had seen us from across the road."

"Yes, as clear and as sure as the sun rose, I saw you and my father behaving ... badly," Laura said quietly, and then sipped the brandy. It was good and warming and so she sipped it again. Laura blinked as if to see if this woman would vanish or change into a husband-stealing harpy before her eyes, but she did not, her countenance did not falter, she was the same elegant female who she had greeted at a distance throughout their relatively brief encounters.

"You saw me say goodbye to Obadiah, Mr Pennington. I apologise for that carelessness, but I had been so worried that he had been caught out in the storm. However, Laura, I will not apologise for loving a man who my own father forbade me to marry."

Laura's head shot up. What was she inferring? How could this genteel lady ever have considered Laura's rough-handed, fisherman father? A tinge of guilt swept through her as she pictured her own, sharp-eyed, fine-featured mother, who rarely smiled anymore, not since Laura was a young child. One lady oozed quiet confidence and warmth, the other a detached air of self-absorption. It was not a loyal thought for a daughter to have, especially one who had just found out her father was a liar…

"He has not explained our story to you, has he?" Mrs King shook her head in seeming disapproval. "Men do not understand how to handle a woman's finer emotions. When they have been 'caught out' they still act and think like naughty boys inside, defensive rather than admitting they may have a failing. Forgive him, Laura."

Laura went to stand up. Forgiveness was not something she could even consider.

"Please, Laura, stay and hear me out. You did the right thing to come to me. I only ask that you listen in an unbiased fashion to what I tell you, for otherwise you may resent me even more than you already do."

Laura could only blink at her, sit back down and sip her brandy. She had not eaten and consequently its warming effect seemed all the more potent. She listened intently as the words washed over her.

"Your father and I go way back. I was the daughter of the man who was the priest in the village church in Alunby along the bay. I fell for the handsome rascal who was always trying to catch my eye from the back pews of the church when we left. He would come into the graveyard at the back of the vicarage and wait for me to appear in the garden at the side of the house and then surprise me. I loved him from the moment he first smiled at me. We would walk, unobserved, amongst the dunes beyond the marshes." Mrs King broke off as she smiled at her private memories. Laura was transfixed, she should have been appalled but this was like listening to a real-life love story. "We became foolish and careless. A parishioner saw me laughing with your father in the old town by his father's boat.

My father was irate. He forbade me to see Obadiah ever again. But Obadiah wanted to prove himself and worked so hard... He toiled night and day to break away from the life he had been born to. He saw how other bay towns further south were evolving and with the money he earned bought a second boat. Then he worked even harder and before long had a third. He sold the catch in Whitby, Scarborough or wherever he could get the best price. If a manor house paid high for a filled order to be delivered as fresh as could be, then he supplied it. My father never cared; Obadiah would always be a peasant fisherman to him."

"Peter was a fisher of men. Did he not know his Bible stories?" Laura snapped out her words in his defence.

"Even priests can have their faults and the sin of pride was one my father suffered dearly from. He loved me but felt that I had had my heart stolen by a common man who should have known his place. So he sent me away, and I was betrothed in my absence to Mr George King of Alunby. My father knew his father, who had been the owner of the funeral directors in Gorebeck. He was the heir of the business but sold it. George was a kind man, who lived in a respectable house at our end of the bay. I had no choice; my alternative was to be sent away to a family member many miles distance from the home I loved, to a spinster aunt in Manchester who had a reputation for being miserly and harsh. To be a companion to such a woman would be like giving up on my own life." She shrugged. "I chose to live a little rather than merely exist."

"I cannot blame you for that," Laura said, as the thought of being trapped at her own mother's side for the rest of her life would be excruciating to her.

"Your father meanwhile did something very brave that helped the whole community. One night, word had it that smugglers were at large in Ebton. A huge fire was started. No one knew why, but Obadiah acted with great bravery and haste. He stopped the village from burning with his quick thinking, saving a number of lives, including my father's young cousin, and through this one act finally earned the gratitude and respect he had been trying so hard to gain for years — but by then I was already wed.

"Your father was a broken man. For months he seemed to lose himself in working even harder. Then your mother latched onto him and in three months he took himself a wife and, well, that was the end of it really, until a few years passed by and my Georgie went out for a ride, met some friends and ended up on the Gorebeck Hunt. The first I knew something was wrong was when they brought him home in the back of a covered wagon. He had taken a heavy fall. His head had been badly bruised and he never recovered." She looked down and Laura could tell that the experience was one that still haunted her. Perhaps she had some affection for her 'Georgie' too. "He died two weeks later and I was asked to leave our house within the week as he had accrued debts. He was a good man but did not know how to live within his means. It was then that the hardest truth was revealed: Georgie had squandered his inheritance away and I had no idea that he had also used the money my father gave him as a marriage settlement. I was penniless overnight.

"Obadiah heard about my situation when he saw the house was up for sale. Always one with an eye for a good deal, he bought it, realising I would be left homeless or sent away to my now even older spinster aunt. He knew that my husband had been a hopeless dreamer who liked to spend and live a life that was too grand for his means. He did not work, you see, never had. Instead he chose to invest, badly as it turned out.

"So Obadiah did the house up and resold it. With the profits he bought this place, changed the rooms so they were suitable for guests, and I was moved in as the landlady. We never planned for our friendship to develop further. He tried to stay true to his wife. Neither of us are wanton adulterers. It just happened that way, as if it was always meant to be, and I ... I cannot say honestly that I have had any regrets, except that we cannot be together all of the time." She glanced nervously at Laura. For the first time her confident countenance wavered. When Laura remained silent, lost to her thoughts, she continued. "Neither of us wanted to break up your family. He would not do anything to hurt you or your mother." She now looked imploringly at Laura.

"Can you not see that you already have done exactly that? You are living a lie. My father preaches to me about propriety and yet comes to your bed under the cover of darkness — how is that not wanton adultery? Mrs King, I think you are deluding yourself." Laura saw the woman's chin rise. She had said words that had hurt and could not take them back, nor did she want to. "It is my mother who is the true victim here. She is left without love and is lonely. What chance does she have to find her heart's desire as she is trapped in a loveless marriage and has been for some considerable time it appears…"

"Oh, please!" The force of Mrs King's words surprised Laura. "Do not be so naïve, Miss Pennington. Forgive me for being so forward, but your mother was and still is a gold digger. She saw the success Obadiah was becoming and what he could still make of himself and, as soon as she could get him out of the old town, she did just that, and in the process moved herself into her own rooms. Yes — her own rooms, not their rooms. He was not allowed to enter her house because he was dirty; a man who risks his life on the high seas to provide for his family was treated by his own wife as a hired help! She would tell him to go to the kitchens of this hotel and enter through there to use the washroom first, to get rid of the smell of fish... Not fit to cross the doorstep to be welcomed into his own home by loving arms.

"Do you think she welcomes him to share her bed? They were man and wife and yet she rejected him. He had one child and you were not a son. Do you think he has had many chances to father one?" Mrs King's hand shot up to her mouth. "I am so sorry, that was beneath me; it was both cruel and crude. I apologise. I must sound so bitter to you. I would never seek to hurt you, Laura, but it was awful to see a man so passionate in nature treated so coldly. He is a gentleman, he would never force her, or demand that she fulfil her marital duties, and she knows this." She swallowed. "This is very forward of me, but it is possibly the only way you can comprehend the sacrifices your father has made. He loves you more than anyone in his life…"

"Except you," Laura said boldly. "You have his heart and soul. I merely have a share in his heart."

Mrs King coloured slightly. "You flatter me but, miss, that is just not true. He would have you live a life away from the prison that your mother makes for you. She would have you docile, obedient and near. If she could find you a husband who merely wanted heirs and was happy for you to be her companion then you would be matched by her to a man of her choosing to suit her lifestyle and not yours. He loves you so much that he wants you to marry a man who will give you the life you desire — even if you do not know that yourself."

"It seems to me that he accuses my mother of wanting to force a marriage of her suiting upon me and yet is that not what he is doing now? He would have me marry a man I do not know at all, but one that suits him," Laura corrected her. At last she had the upper hand.

The woman opposite her smiled knowingly. "But that is not true, is it, Miss Laura? You do know Mr Daniel Tranton, or are at least acquainted with him because you and the boy are waiting for him to return, are you not?"

Laura was lost for words. "You know of Jeb?" she asked, but then cringed as she had said his name and therefore admitted her part in hiding him.

"I found him curled up in my back yard earlier this morning. The boat he had been hiding in had been moved. Your father had left already and I realised he was cold, hungry and scared."

"Where is he now?" Laura was scared that he had been sent to the poorhouse.

"Young Jeb is fast asleep in my kitchen by a warm fire. He told me you helped him and that Mr Tranton will come back for him. The very same Mr Daniel Tranton who is your father's friend and choice for you, if I am not mistaken."

Laura ignored her comment. "I have received word that Mr Tranton has his papers, so Jeb is no longer hunted. He is now Mr Daniel Tranton's apprentice. Can I tell him and can you keep him safely here, please? I need to find my father. I must speak with him, urgently."

"Very well, we shall put his mind at rest. His arm looks like it is healing well. I have given him a new salve. He should be restored now." She sat back and looked at Laura as if she was contemplating saying more, but Laura had had far too many revelations for one morning.

"Thank you." Laura stood up.

"Do you have anything else you would like to say to me? If you wish to berate me, then this is your chance, Laura. I shall not allow it again. I do have standards and I shall hold my head high, for all I have done is care for the man I have always loved and yet can never fully have. But I will have what I can of him."

The ironic vows: 'To have and to hold' echoed in Laura's unspoken thoughts.

Laura shook her head. "You have chosen your path and acted accordingly. Now I must do the same. I must find Father. Good day, Mrs King, and thank you for at least offering up an explanation. It is not the time for me to comment for you may have been familiar with your circumstances for years and have made arrangements to fit a lifestyle that is acceptable to you both; however, I have just learned of this 'situation'. So I will need time to be able to fathom it ... as for acceptance, that is also something I feel I need more time for."

"Laura." Mrs King said quickly. "I know this is a huge shock to you but please speak kindly to your father; his only sin is to find true love when any form of love was denied him by his wife. He will never turn her out or divorce her. But she broke his heart; he stayed with her because of his love for you. Please, let him be truly happy again." She paused and then, almost as she was uncertain of whether she should talk further, she spoke her mind. "Should we be friends, Miss Laura Pennington? I have never, and never would try to take your father's love away from you. His heart is big enough to love us both. I was never blessed with a child of my own. It would appear I am quite barren."

The older woman stood. There was sadness in her words that was reflected in her eyes. She offered Laura her hand.

Laura nodded. She found she had no wish to hurt or insult her further. "We should be polite acquaintances, because to be enemies would only cause Father greater pain and neither of us want that, do we?" Laura did not shake her hand. It was too soon to be so forgiving and accepting. She only had Mrs King's word that what she had said about their past and her mother was true. Convincing as it was, she could not be so easily persuaded to take her father's mistress's side against her mother. Mrs King may very well be the reason why her mother was so bitter, she thought.

"No," Mrs King replied. "That we do not."

Laura forced a polite smile onto her face. It would take time to know and to trust these two people again, her father especially, as she had held him in such high regard throughout her life.

"I would like to see Jeb for myself if you do not mind," she said abruptly.

"Very well," Mrs King replied.

Laura was led through to the kitchen where Jeb was curled up in the chair, fast asleep.

"Jeb," Laura said, and the boy awoke and stood straight away, smiling at her. "You are no longer hunted."

He almost jumped with joy. "I'm free!" he said.

"Yes, but Mr Daniel Tranton owns your papers and you shall be his apprentice until you are old enough to make your own path in life. He will look after you fairly, of that I am sure for he has your best interests at heart. He is not like his cousin."

"Thank you, miss," he said, nodding in answer to her question.

Satisfied that he was indeed safe, Laura left.

Chapter 7

Laura ran down to the old town as fast as she could, ignoring her desire to go and demand answers from her mother and find out if she knew about Mrs King. Surely she could not. Laura could not fathom how to broach the subject to her. They did not converse easily at the best of times and these were about the worst that Laura could imagine. Could any woman live contentedly, knowing that her husband was having a liaison with a neighbour? And especially one that was in his employ?

She ran down to the line of cobles but her father was nowhere to be seen so she broke another one of his orders and made her way to the inn. She dared not enter the tap room but skirted around the back. Old Amy occasionally sat on an upturned barrel mending nets there, but instead of Amy she saw her father talking to a tall, bearded man wearing knee-high cavalry boots that matched a wide leather belt. Realising that it was Arnold Glynn, the gamekeeper of Hamiltons' estate, who must have returned early from Gorebeck, she stayed hidden. He cut a striking figure, not one many would like to come across if trespassing. It had never occurred to her that he might come back earlier than expected.

"I tell you, Obadiah, the men are a gathering and there will be a trap set for him." The man's voice was gruff but clear. Her father looked very concerned, anxious even. She had stopped at the edge of the inn and nestled behind a stack of three large hogsheads to listen.

"This cannot be. He is a good man. I've known young Daniel Tranton for years. I taught him to fish, how to track and how to be a real man, not a prissy fop as his mother would have had him be. Now, his cousin is a different kettle of fish — I could understand it if they were setting their sights on that cruel bastard. He pays them a pittance and only gives them time to get over illness if they cannot stand, but Daniel — no, you must be mistaken. Either you misheard, or they have the wrong man, or the wrong mill."

Laura's ears did not deceive her. There was a threat to Daniel Tranton and his mill. He did not deserve that. Neither did she deserve being offered up to his 'cruel bastard' of a cousin!

Arnold continued, "But that's just it — they ain't real machine wreckers. I worked over in the west for Hamilton. Believe me, he could make Mr Roderick Tranton look like a guardian angel the things he done. The man's family made money from the slaves in the West Indies for generations first, so they know how to work folk like dogs. But these men don't speak like they're from West Yorkshire, they're returners from the wars like Bullman and his cronies. There's only about five of them, but you don't need more than that to whip up a crowd. Panic and indignation spread quickly as food would to hungry bellies. I tell you we'll be in the national newspapers this time next month. We'll have the militia brought in to quash any more trouble. That's not good for any of us, is it?"

Obadiah shook his head. "No, you're right, but Daniel's folk aren't starving, are they?"

"That's not the reason they're a watching him."

"What is then?" Obadiah asked.

"I reckon they either want his mill or they seek the destruction of it and Mr Daniel Tranton stands square in their way."

Obadiah thought for a moment. "Well, we'll stop them. You can tell your master that his boat has been made ready and is on the beach waiting to go with his things still hidden safe within it. But Hamilton is out of his mind. Why would anyone from the west come for him here? What evil deed did he do that made him move across the land to escape these people — whoever they are? What of his daughter? Is she to be chased across the water too like a refugee? The man has an oar loose, I tell you. God's help will be needed if it is the results of his own evil that he runs from."

"I think it is, maybe only he knows the truth of what haunts him, but these men that have arrived have nought to do with him. Hamilton has the shadow of his conscience hanging over him, definitely. Why not let the bugger run and take his chances? He has done nought but fence off our land and stop us from going where our folks have trod for generations. Let him run, I say, and good riddance. He does not need to know that they are Ivor Bullman's henchmen and they do not have him or Gorebeck Mill as the target of their venom, but Mr Daniel Tranton's mill." He dropped his hat on the barrel at the back of the inn. "It's damned thirsty work snooping around the countryside after these buggers. Have an ale with me, Obadiah, like you used to?"

"Thank you, Arnold, for telling me all this." Her father looked up at the sky as Laura had seen him do so many times when seeking to catch an idea or for inspiration to come to him. "I would love to sit and drink with you, my friend, but there is much to consider."

"Obadiah, word has it that they are not only planning to damage the mill, but to hurt Daniel, too. I don't know if this is to do with his wallet or him personally, but if he is a good man then perhaps we need to intervene sooner rather than later."

"So what is in all this for Bullman?" Obadiah asked.

"Control. He can twist Roderick Tranton around his little finger because the man is scared of him and hides within his ledgers. He may even have unwittingly got his backing to remove Daniel Tranton. Bullman would stop at nothing to get his way; the question is how far would Roderick Tranton knowingly go?"

"But to harm his cousin and take what is not his — if inheriting is what he seeks — it's nothing short of murder!" Obadiah said in incredulity. Then somewhat calmer he continued, "We must be careful about what we say, we are making assumptions we cannot back up. I'll ride over tomorrow and warn Daniel myself. We have time on our side if the meeting is not till Monday. This is a bad business, but keep it quiet."

Arnold Glynn agreed, grabbed his hat and left.

Her father entered the back of the inn after watching Glynn make his way up the steep headland path onto Hamiltons' land. Laura found it difficult to comprehend that her father could even think of drinking at a time like this. He should be doing something — warning Daniel Tranton now! If she heard correctly, he was in grave danger of being attacked. Her father was most likely worn out by all his shenanigans, she thought uncharitably, so she would have to take matters into her own hands. She had saved Jeb, now she must save Mr Daniel Tranton and in so doing, she would save his mill also.

Laura returned home and made her riding outfit ready for an early morning outing. She would not take her dinner with her mother or father if he decided to return, instead she would stay in her own rooms and have soup brought as if she was feeling unwell. Her mother would leave her alone. She had no worries on that score.

Her mother had insisted that she was taught how to ride, so that when they had the carriage to go regularly to the assembly rooms, Laura would be able to quote riding as one of her accomplishments, along with her pleasant singing voice and fine needlepoint. Laura managed to master riding side-saddle. She did not find it the most comfortable way of sitting atop a horse, but it was respectable and bearable. Laura had loved riding, using her father's saddle the most, experiencing the freedom of letting an animal gallop along the flat sandy bay. She was as a free spirit trying to take flight. Her father had heartily disapproved. He said the beasts were untrustworthy, having fallen off one in his younger days. He could ride but did not enjoy it as he would rather be in control of his coble. Laura's joy had been short-lived as Obadiah had the horse stabled at the hotel. It was frequently hired out to guests and another attempt of her mother to move one step nearer owning two horses and a carriage had been thwarted. Obadiah had informed Laura that she had looked like she was a wild, mad woman racing the horse along the flat sandy beach.

When morning broke, suitably attired, Laura went down to the back of the hotel. The lad that tended the stable and saw to fetching and carrying for Mrs King was busy stacking logs in the barn.

"Saddle Misty for me," Laura ordered.

"Yes, miss…" He hesitated after stacking the last log on top of the pile.

"Well? What are you waiting for?" she asked, staring directly at him.

"Er, does Mrs King know that you are here, miss? I mean she didn't ask me to get him ready and…" He looked anxiously around the yard at the back of the house as if the woman was going to appear. This Laura definitely hoped would not happen. She had no wish to see the lady — the woman — again for some time.

"Do you know who I am?" she snapped.

"No," he answered honestly, and flinched when she answered.

"Miss Pennington. My father owns the horse, the stable, the hotel and therefore pays your wages as he does Mrs King's!"

"Sorry, sorry, didn't know, miss," he said and ran inside the stall and saddled the animal, quickly as he could, then emerged leading the horse out behind him.

"Thank you." Laura quickly mounted Misty, tossed the chastened lad a coin and rode off straight for the Gorebeck moor road. From there she could take the route down toward Daniel's mill and, well, how difficult could it be to locate it? She just had to follow the road from Gorebeck to Beckton, staying by the river.

Annie saw Laura ride out and threw the cloth she had been using to wipe down the window on the floor. The moisture inside each morning was a pain, like the range that needed blacking, the rugs that needed beating, the food that needed preparing and the woman who constantly needed tending. What was Laura bloody Pennington up to now? Annie watched her go at speed down the road towards Gorebeck moor. She had had more than enough of keeping the secrets of this family and now her old friend did not even share with her what was happening. Something was up and with it was Annie's patience. She worked harder here for them than she had helping her ma with the nets and gutting fish. Well, she sniffed, perhaps it weren't as bad as gutting fish, but still Laura should have told her what she was about. At one time they had kept every secret between them that the small village held.

Now she was Laura Pennington's servant! Well, servants gossip, don't they, she thought. She knew something most certainly was up and if Laura was above sharing it with her then Laura could be brought back down a peg or two like that fool of a mother of hers.

She took off her apron, dropped it on the chair then stormed out of the house. If she was to be treated in such an off-hand manner then it was time she shared a few things with her own mother.

The old cottage door was ajar as always.

"Ma!" Annie shouted and was instantly greeted by her mother, who was frantically wiping her hands on her already stained apron as she came forward to hug her daughter.

"Aren't you a treat for sore eyes! I've got a pot of broth brewing, you sit yersel' down and I'll get it. You work so hard. How's Glad? Still being waspish, is she? She'll settle, you'll see... Might pop and see her tomorrow when there's a fresh catch in…"

"Ma, stop chattering and take breath, please. I need to talk to you, quiet like." Annie saw the sparkle in the older woman's eyes, she loved a gossip and there was often something happening amongst the bay towns.

Ivy closed the door instantly, took a seat next to her daughter on a three-legged stool and was all ears. She took Annie's hand and said, "What is it love? Can you tell me, is Glad … ill?"

"It's nothing bad, Ma. Well not for me, or you, but I think you should know the truth of it before you hear it from someone else."

"That sounds bad enough, lass," her mother said.

"It's about Mr Obadiah Pennington, his lordship," she said and sneered, but her mother raised a warning finger at her disrespect and so she quickly continued. "He is not as good a man as you and Pa think he is."

"Now, lass, you don't bite the hand that feeds you, do you?"

"I know he has a fancy woman and I don't think it is something I should be keeping quiet about. At least not with you." She saw her mother's face change from concern to shock.

Ivy sat up, straight-backed. "What do you know of such things?" she asked.

"I know enough to recognise when a man is not sleeping in his wife's bed, but instead is creeping around in the small hours of the morning, that something is very wrong with the marriage ... and them supposed to be so God fearing!" Annie thought that her voice conveyed just the right note of disgust. She tried to hide the glee that was building within her. Her mother had not known this gossip before her, that was a first!

"Poor Glad," her mother said and it was Annie's turn to look shocked. "She's all alone, Annie. I must speak to her. Tell me, who is this Jezebel?"

"Mrs King, Ma," Annie revealed in a slow voice to emphasize her worth at divulging such a secret. "And she always acts so proper like." She stifled the smile that had threatened to spread across her face.

Ivy grabbed her shawl.

"Where you going, Ma?" Annie asked.

"To sort our Glad out, that's where," Ivy replied.

"But, Ma, I have to get back. I'll be missed. I only wanted you to know, in case ought was said," Annie said as she began to stand up.

"No, lass. You stay put until I come back and don't tell a soul about this, especially your Pa!"

Annie was going to protest but her mother had gone.

"Damn!" Annie said, and sunk back down into her mother's chair, angered at the injustice of it all. Why should her mother and father toil so? Their world had only changed marginally with the addition of her own wages, meanwhile the Penningtons' domination of the town was spreading out along the bay. When would enough be enough for them? They brought in strangers, richer strangers, who looked down on them – her villagers, her friends and family, the people who valued Ebton and who had ancestors going back generations in the area. If she did not stop Obadiah then the whole of the bay would fall to his hedonistic ways. Well, as she sat back in the chair near the warm hearth sipping her mother's broth, she happily reflected that times were about to change.

Chapter 8

Mrs King walked out of the back of the building just after midday. She saw Ivy from the village entering the back of the Pennington's' place and waved at her. The woman cut her dead. Strange, she thought, she was normally such a friendly type. Perhaps that daughter of hers had riled her again. Obadiah had not wanted to take Annie on, said she was a bad influence on Laura, but her mother and father had been their friends and so he had felt obligated.

She had no more time to think about Ivy's odd behaviour as she saw the stable lad sweeping out the stall and looked around puzzled. The one thing that was missing was the horse. "Where is Misty?" she asked him.

"Not back yet," he answered, as he diligently swept away.

"Not back yet from where?" she said, rather surprised. Her smile faltered as she asked the question.

"Miss Pennington hasn't come back from her ride, miss. She said the horse belonged to her pa, and that he allowed her to exercise it, so I thought... Have I done something wrong, Mrs King?" His big eyes stared hopefully at her. He was not the brightest lamp in the room, but Mrs King knew he had a good heart and an elderly mother who relied on the lad's wage to make ends meet.

"No, Henry, it is not you who has done anything wrong. You only did what Miss Pennington knew you would, that's all." She smiled at him even though anger prickled at her normal calm demeanour. If Laura had taken Misty out of spite ... then, no, surely not. Laura was hurting but she did not strike Mrs King as a vengeful person. She sighed deeply. What on earth was happening to this place, she wondered. Their normally predictable routine was being completely upturned. In the middle of it was a young woman, who had had her world pulled inside out by the person she was closest to, her own father. Laura worshipped him as if he was perfect; poor Obie, he was only a man not a god.

Henry was watching her, unsure if he should continue with his task or not.

"You run down to the inn, Henry, and see if Mr Pennington is there. If he is, ask him if he could come by the hotel as Miss Pennington is still out on her ride and he said that he wanted to catch her when she returns."

Henry ran off.

Something was wrong, very wrong, because no one took 'the nag' out, as Obadiah called it, unless it was her, or she rented it out through the hotel. Whatever that girl was about, it was definitely without her father's consent. She only hoped that the naïve young woman had not taken it into her head to run away because of the recent revelations. Mrs King returned to her parlour and waited patiently for the tornado of Obadiah Pennington to blow in. It would be a hard task, but she would have to calm him down before he would be able to think straight and decide what to do. That would be her challenge for the day, but if anyone could, Mrs King knew fine well it was her.

Ivy entered the Pennington's' home through the back of the house.

"Glad!" she called out as she took in how fancy and fine the place was. Ivy thought that she now understood why Gladys was so taken with it all that she did not want to leave it to come down to the old cottages that stunk of fish nets, sand

and salt. There was no answer to her call so she went up a few steps and into the parlour where Annie had told her that Gladys sat most of the day, lost in her own fantasy world of grandeur. The lass was wrong — this was no fantasy, this was real, thought Ivy, as she pushed the door open. The sad truth was, though, that Glad was about to have a wakeup call, and it would break her new world in two. If it was the end of her friendship, then so be it, but Ivy would tell the woman for her own good.

"Glad, dear," Ivy said, as she entered the carpeted room. She had wiped most of the sand from her boots on the rug in the kitchen so she had not left too much of a trail going into the house.

"Ivy! What are you doing here?" Gladys Pennington said, sitting straight in her chair. "Where's Annie? Has something happened to the girl?"

"No, she's fine."

"Then why are you here?"

Ivy did not rebuke her but answered with a faint smile playing on her lips, even if the sentiment was not reflected in her eyes. "I've come because it's time we talked, love. You've not been yourself since that doctor gave you that laudynum stuff. You don't need that, it's no good. You need to see and listen clear like. So Ivy's brought you some of her special brew and you sit and do listen good to what I have to tell you." She held out a bottle to her friend.

Gladys Pennington was hesitant. But she licked her lips, and then Ivy knew how much she had missed it as she reached for the bottle. Etiquette temporarily forgotten, she swigged her friend's best brew as she always used to, before licking her lips as if taking nectar into her mouth and savouring every drop.

"See, now you remember what you've been missing. Oh, love, this is a fine place, but it lacks soul — yours. What's happened? I thought you'd be happy up here in your palace. You have to make a house a home, not a prison." Ivy words were direct as always.

"You've always lacked social graces, Ivy. So what is it you want to tell me? Spit it out. I know you too well to mess with my words." Gladys Pennington stared at her through slightly blurred eyes.

"You best brace yourself, Glad. It's about Obadiah and his shenanigans."

"What's he been up to now?" She took another long swig of the brew.

"He's not being true to you, Glad. I'm sorry, love, but word is out and I don't want you to hear from no one else. He'll make you the talk of the bay — a laughingstock, and I will not stand by and let him. Not now you've something to be proud about."

"Word is out about what? You speak in riddles woman. Where is that lazy daughter of yours?" She looked past Ivy to the doorway. Clearly agitated, she was trying to avoid the issue.

"There's a secret that Obadiah has being keeping from you, but he cannot anymore. He's been seen and, well, tongues wag." Ivy stuck to her task.

"Spit it out, whatever you have heard — is it from that old blatherskite Amy down in the Coble Inn? Or have you merely come here to gloat, is that it, because you've heard the gossip?" Mrs Pennington's tired eyes finally focussed on her old friend's face.

"Now, you know Ivy better than that, don't you? But if blunt is what you want then blunt is what I give you: he's been having an affair and right under your nose, if not under your roof — but under one of his own! And no, Amy don't know nothing from me — whether she knows it yet or not I have no inkling as I'm not about to ask her and spread the muck even further, am I?" Ivy shook her head, disappointed at the accusation that she would take delight in breaking her friend's heart and shattering her dreams.

"Ivy... Ivy... Do you not think I don't know it already?" Gladys asked and stared into the fire's dying flames. "He's not interested in me... Hasn't been for years. He's only interested in being rich. Neither is he interested in being a fine gentleman, so he does his social climbing in bed atop 'a lady', or so he thinks. She's nothing. She had a good husband and heartlessly sent him to his early grave and now she wants to have mine." Gladys Pennington continued staring at the flames as if hypnotised by them.

"Oh, lass, you knew it all along!" Ivy was shocked. Then she understood as realisation dawned. "That is why you sit here moping all day and sleeping as much as you can. You've let yourself be dulled and drugged with that stuff!" Ivy said bitterly.

Gladys nodded. "I had such dreams for us, me and my Obadiah, and just when it is all coming together, he is blowing it all apart." She sniffed.

Ivy crossed her arms across her bosom. "Right, well he's not having it all his own way. I'm going to be taking over Annie's work and getting you off that laudynum stuff. You are going to have a companion from the minute you wake to the minute you sleep. You are going to be seen promenading along the seafront and taking the air. You are going to interest yourself in the management of the bathing machines for them ladies and gentlemen he is trying to attract." Ivy rattled out her plan.

"I'm not going in the sea, I'll catch dropsy!" Gladys Pennington looked as though she would run away at the very thought of it.

"Not use them but find out how they is supposed to be good for you. Then take a trip to Harrogate, there's a spa there. You can advertise the waters of Ebton. Tell Obadiah 'your' vision. How you will mingle and gain favour with the idle who have nought better to think of than how to extend their empty lives. You will engage with Obadiah's plans and you will be the wife he used to have who still thinks straight."

"But, Ivy, you thought of this, I do not have his vision." Gladys Pennington's eyes brightened, became watery, but her face showed her fear and caution.

"Aye, well I will get you going, but you know how to put on them airs and graces and once you are off the drug then you can build on the ideas yourself. Right now you have to act more alert than perhaps you are feeling. We have to get Glad back in the game. Annie can do my work in the village and we shall plan, you and me. First, though, you must tell me a very important point: do you want Obadiah back as your husband, or not? If not, then we must be canny and find out how you can bring him down and raise you and Laura up in the world — do whatever you can. He is an adulterer and you and she are innocent " Ivy winked at her.

"What of poor Laura, the stigma on her if we separate would be too much. She may marry soon. It would ruin her chances and there is such a good match in the offing."

"Well, poor Laura will be alright then. What if you find out what you can have and threaten his business? If he does not provide all you wish for then you threaten to take advice from a man of law and to hell with his plans for marrying his precious daughter off. Her and Annie were so close, now she doesn't even chatter with the lass. Do you know how lonely my Annie is and how hurtful that attitude of Laura's is?" Ivy stressed the point by leaning forward, but Gladys instantly shrank back and stared blankly at her friend and swallowed. "So do you still want him?" Ivy repeated.

"No, not back in my bed, but I won't divorce him, not yet." Gladys Pennington sat up straight, confidence restored, anger and revenge simmering inside a refocused mind.

"Why, if he is keeping you tied to a marriage that you do not want. You are still young enough to find another husband, a better man," Ivy said.

"I don't want one! They always disappoint. You cannot trust men — they are selfish and the older they get the more so they become. I want grandchildren. If I divorce him he is free to wed his whore and I do not want that. Why should he be happy and her a respectable wife with my man, when I cannot be? No, I will see Laura wed and I will be near her. I will live separately to him, avoid him, but I will never free him. He can carry the sin to his grave and she can live in the knowledge that 'Mrs King' is no better than a common fisherman's whore! People will look and see her for what she is and her hotel will take on the mantle of a house of low morals, then where will he put her when it affects his growing trade?" Her words were sharp and her wits, likewise, were still there when provoked.

"You have thought this through in some detail, haven't you, lass. What is it they say about revenge being bittersweet?" Ivy asked.

"I do not care what 'they say' but he soon will." She laughed, an empty hollow sound. "Oh yes, what else do you think I stay up here mulling over day in and day out, but I have been waiting for my Laura to wed, to free me. She must, and then all can be put right. Until then I am completely trapped. But Ivy, you are welcome here for I need you to be my eyes, ears and ... if it is not too late for you to be my friend…"

"When did I ever stop being that, Glad?"

Ivy hugged Gladys Pennington and the woman let her, even though her response was awkward and light and when the woman stopped crying she sat up straight, wiped her eyes and replied, "You never did. I'm so sorry, Ivy."

"You've took me job!" Annie was livid with her mother.

"Aye, for now. You help out here and see to your pa. I need to see to things up at the house." Ivy was controlling her anger but her daughter's tone was one she would not accept.

"No! It is your job to be with Pa. I need to keep an eye on what Laura is up to. Mrs Pennington always moans at me. I should not have told you!" Annie opened the cottage door but she was not quick enough as Ivy slammed the door shut and rounded on her.

"Now listen, Annie, and listen good. You've told me this secret because your nose was put right out of joint by Laura's high-handedness, no doubt at the insistence of her ma. If I let you run around with gossip that will bring about the ruin of Obadiah's plans then what next?"

Annie shrugged. "He'll become a fisherman again and his fine ideas will crumble. Laura will have to return and she'll need her old friend back!"

"You bleedin' little idiot! He will fall and his businesses will too. Like his little fleet of cobles that your pa depends upon for our living. So you think you can turn back time to how it was before they built that row of terraces of houses on the lower cliff? You don't understand it, do you, Annie? If Obadiah has to sell out or move away then strangers will still come in. Someone will buy the new houses and look on our part of town and say it's an eyesore. They'll stop the fishing for tours. They might even drive us out. What would they care for the boats — for our livelihoods. How would you like to have to work in Gorebeck Mill, eh? Can't you see that it is best to control the devil you know than have him replaced with one that cares nothing about the locals. Obadiah might be tupping the King woman, but he is one of us and he pays your pa better than most. If they are shunned and driven out then what he has begun will be taken over by worse than he."

"Aren't you angry with your old 'friend', Ma?" Annie asked.

"Oh yes, Annie, I am. Who likes to be shunned? But I also know that she needs help and a friend in need is a friend indeed. Once I've bailed her out of the rut she is wallowing in she won't be able to cast Ivy off so easily again," Ivy said and smiled at her daughter.

Annie brightened. "See, I was right to tell you — I knew you'd have a plan!"

"Ah, lass, you'll learn yet. Now I need me other dress and then she'll see that her companion needs a new outfit if she is to be seen in public with her." Ivy's smile spread across her face. She had not had anything new for years; ah, one woman's fall was another woman's rise.

Daniel was approaching Gorebeck when he saw three figures loitering by the side of the road ahead of him. One was standing, one was crouching and the other was half laid down, resting back on his elbows on the grassy bank.

The man standing stepped into the road in front of him as he approached. His attire was different to that of the locals; he had a tall hat, a long grey jacket and dark tweed trousers. To Daniel, he looked like a troublemaker so he kept his distance as he slowed his trotting horse to a standstill.

He began to approach Daniel with his hands raised slightly as if to show he meant no harm. Daniel was not convinced by this half-hearted gesture. He glanced behind at the other two who were both now sitting up, watching.

"Now then, mister." Tall hat's voice was loud, confident and to Daniel it showed barely veiled arrogance.

"Now what?" Daniel asked, remaining at a distance, trying to keep the horse and himself out of the stranger's arm's reach.

"Me and my colleagues, we've come here looking for work."

"Many men have. What has this to do with me?" Daniel replied.

"Served our time, paid our dues to King and country and now need to live, but on what? You wouldn't know where we would find any jobs, would you?" The man spoke clearly, educated definitely, with no hint of a local accent. He was a cut above the men Ivor Bullman usually associated with, but his two friends were true to type.

"You best try in town," Daniel offered, then added, "I suppose it depends upon what kind of work you seek?" Daniel wondered if they had picked him out because he was gentry or because they were waiting for him specifically. The other two men got to their feet. Daniel was thinking the latter was the case.

He wished he had his rifle with him as he had when he was a skirmisher in Spain. Making a break from these three would have been easy then, but he was unarmed and he wondered if the same could be said for them.

"We are looking for work, mill work, like many in these parts and in the cities, but they don't hire anymore, do they?" The man folded his arms in front of him and stared at Daniel.

"Then you best try the farms, there is usually work in the fields to do at this time of year and it is a damned sight healthier for you than the dry or dusty work in the mills."

Daniel tugged at the reins to steer his horse past them, when he noticed one of the men on the verge pulling something from his coat pocket. These men were seeking him out; they could be part of the rabble brought in to target him and his mill. Had he been a fool by riding out on his own? Sleights had warned him and yet he had still left himself open to attack. His mind was clear as to the danger, but his options were very limited. Which one was the weaker? Could he ride at the man in front and make it into Gorebeck?

"Oh, I don't think we are cut out for the farms. We're men of action and right now we are going to take action against the oppressors…"

"How so?" A few seconds passed by that seemed to drag on like minutes, but then Daniel heard pounding and realised it was not his heart, but the noise of another horse's hooves thundering along the road approaching Gorebeck bridge.

Daniel sighed with relief as the man's hand returned into his pocket, and the other men stepped back, but relief turned to amazement when he realised that the rider was none other than Miss Pennington, riding at speed toward him.

"Mr Tranton," she shouted.

The men melted as shadows, drifting away along a footpath that took them off down by the river's tow path.

Laura stopped her horse next to Daniel's. He automatically put out a hand to steady her as she pulled up quickly. He smiled happily to see her. Daniel had been released from a trap by this beautiful woman, so full of life and energy. She was so different to the pale faces he was introduced to at the side of their mothers when he was forced to socialise at gatherings where he was expected to mingle and seek out a wife.

"Miss Pennington, we must enter the town, and quickly. Please come with me now for we are not safe here." He led her horse around so that they could ride back into Gorebeck and away from the open road.

"Very well, let us move quickly for I have some important news, Mr Tranton," she said. Laura rode alongside him into Gorebeck where they quickly dismounted, and she allowed him to escort her into the lounge of the Hare and Rabbit.

Inside the dimly lit lounge, he led her to a corner table, which was partially screened by a potted fern, and ordered a drink to calm both of them.

"Mr Tranton," she began, "you must listen to me and take my words very seriously."

He stared back at her, mesmerised by her concerned expression.

"You are in great danger," she blurted out. "There are some awful men coming to your mill to hurt you. They're not what they claim to be and … they will be like wolves acting as sheep, but you must be on your guard! I do not have names... I do not understand why because your cousin apparently is a much worse man than you but they have decided to hurt you…"

Laura pulled off her riding gloves and placed them on her lap. She looked relieved to have shared the information with him. Her hands rested delicately on each other.

Daniel leaned forward and gently took hold of her left hand; her fingers were small and delicate against his. Laura did not pull away but swallowed as she looked into his eyes.

"How do you know this?"

"Mr Arnold Glynn, Hamiltons' gamekeeper, told my father that these men, whoever they are, are coming here for you. I do not know when or how but please take my words seriously. Father was going to leave it to come till the morning because he said nothing would happen before some meeting on Monday."

"So why, dear Laura, are you here now?" he asked, still gently holding her fingers in his palm.

"I decided that that might be too late. I mean, if it was known already that they were planning something awful for you, how could anyone think they would wait for a meeting to put their plan into place? So I decided I would try to reach you today. It may have been a rash act, and he will be very angry with me, but I make no apology for it. The fact that we met on the road is surely a sign I acted in the best interest... It seems to me, Daniel, that you and I are meant to work together in some way to prevent an even greater wrong than that which nearly befell young Jeb. Perhaps you are correct in your assumption about fate." She smiled to try and break the tension. She gently pulled her fingers free and patted the back of his hand before glancing anxiously around lest someone should be observing them.

"You could not have arrived at a better moment ... fate again or destiny."

"I do not understand, Mr Tranton," she said. "I did nothing other than meet you."

"Those men by the roadside were going to hurt me, Laura, and your intervention prevented them from doing so. You have already saved me from an attack, without even realising it. You are a very special person. I am indeed in your debt again, as I was for hiding Jeb. If it is affection I show it is truly sincere."

"Then I would ask that you separate your gratitude from affection as they are two very different emotions," she said, as she saw his fingers relax.

"I apologise. I behave badly."

Laura instantly held his hand. "No, not that, I mean I like the sound of being your sweet … well, I meant, what did I interrupt?"

He smiled at her as he gently stroked the back of her hand, sending a wave of exciting sensations through Laura's body that appeared to remove all her confusion and anxiety in one warm rush. This had been the most demanding of days and yet, sitting opposite Daniel in their own little oasis of calm, it was rapidly becoming the best and most exciting one she had ever known.

"The three men, Laura, were about to either ambush or hurt me. There was no one else around and I unwittingly rode straight into them. I had no weapon on me and no way of raising an alarm for I was too far away from the town to be heard."

Laura looked at the man opposite. His eyes at that moment were vulnerable, and she could not bear to lose him before they had the chance to discover the joy of each other's company. Her father may have singled him out, and that alone was good enough reason for her to reject him, but she could not in all honesty look at him and not see him as someone she would like to know better — a lot better. Right now she could think of no other person she would rather spend her time with.

"We should go to the militia! We must have them all arrested and imprisoned," Laura said.

"It is not that simple, Laura. They have not done or said anything wrong at the moment and I cannot have men arrested for merely thinking they may be about to do some evil deed. It is not enough to suspect them, or accuse them, and simply have them rounded up. No, Laura, unfortunately I need proof and although I know who is behind them — Mr Ivor Bullman — I need to seek out the proof that will incriminate him too." He sat back in his chair as their tea arrived. "Where is Jeb?" he asked, as he sipped the warm liquid from the china cup.

"He is in the safe keeping of a woman called Mrs King who runs the hotel for Father." She could not help it, her manner had changed — her words became abrupt, a bitter tone hung in the air that even her own ears picked up on.

"Something troubles you about her?" he asked and leaned forward a little.

"She is nice enough, if you like her kind ... well, I know she will keep him safe. What are we to do about those men then?" she asked, not wanting to explain further.

"You, Laura, are not doing anything. You have done more than enough already. I shall book you a room here for you cannot return home today."

"Mr Tranton, I came here to help you and I intend to see this through. I will not be told what I can and cannot do like a child would be."

"Laura, listen to me please. I will not see you hurt. You are brave, yes. But there is a time to be wise also. These men are violent. There may be more of them. I am an ex-solider. I have others amongst my mill workers. Please step back now, bury that pride of yours and allow me to do what I must. I promise I will come back here and tell you all." He was not smiling.

"You give me your word, Daniel?" Laura asked, reluctantly seeing he was right. She may be able to ride and deliver messages, but what did she know about the rabble and fighting? Nothing! But she remembered the fear she felt when the shot had rung out over her head only days before.

"I must see my cousin. I will then have to decide what to do and if the militia should be involved or the magistrate." Daniel looked at her and raised an eyebrow as if waiting for her agreement.

"Very well. My father will be very angry with me, I fear," Laura admitted, but did not look at all guilty. "I cannot stay here as I have nothing with me. Neither do I have the money to pay for the room myself. It appears that I have placed myself in an awkward situation."

"My credit is good here; I will have anything you need placed on my account." Daniel stood up.

Laura laughed. "No, that cannot be. Whatever would people say? I will just have to annoy Father further and place my purchases upon his account. May as well be hanged for a sheep as a lamb," she said.

"Why do I get the impression that you are not at all concerned whether your father is angry with you, or not?" he asked.

"Perhaps because he ... well just let us say, that if you preach high morals and good behaviour you should make sure that you set a good example yourself. Besides, although he is usually a very honourable and astute man, his decision to delay coming to you was very wrong."

Daniel nodded. "On that I would heartily agree."

"Please take a weapon with you, Daniel. You need to be armed."

He smiled at her concern and left.

Chapter 9

Obadiah stormed into the hotel and headed straight for the parlour to find Mrs King. "What has she done now?" he demanded to know.

"Calm down, please, Obie. I don't know exactly. I only found out that she had ridden off earlier and has not returned. I have no idea what she has in mind, but she had no baggage with her and was apparently dressed in the appropriate attire for a ride out. I had not seen her since she left here after we had an earnest discussion about our 'friendship'. That was yesterday when she went in search of you. She was quite polite, considering, and did not seem that distressed, but she was shocked. I have no idea if she went to see her mother or just tried to find you."

"She came here? You spoke with her openly about us?" He looked incredulous. "Did she hurl insults at you?"

"How little you know your own daughter, Obie," Mrs King said, and noticed a tired, guilty look in his eyes. The lines around his eyes that she was so used to from years spent on the sea in all weathers, somehow seemed deeper.

"I've been busy providing for her and her mother all these years. You of all people know how hard I work. She was always such a headstrong child." He looked away. "How many ways can a man be pulled?" he asked and stared down at his feet. "She should have been a son — then she could have helped me with my businesses instead of worrying me into my grave!"

"Obie." Mrs King placed her hands on his upper arms and stood close to him. "Don't take on so. I have never pulled you in any direction that your heart did not want you to go and you know that. Laura is a woman and not a child, one day she was bound to find out. Better to gain her acceptance and try to rebuild that damaged, but not quite broken place, that is her heart." She kissed his cheek tenderly.

"You think she will understand?" Obadiah asked, clearly doubting that it would be possible. "She knows nothing of love, passion, lust … of the essence of life itself."

"No, nor should she, yet. You nurtured and encouraged her to be outgoing and adventurous. She is part of you, but more than that she is her own person. Laura can see how sad you are with her mother. She may not have wanted to acknowledge the truth, but it was before her to see. She loves you, Obie, she will only want what was best for you. You raised her to be out there in Life, in the boat, in the world, before your grand ideas took off. Now you expect her to sit in the parlour with her mama all day long listening to the woman bemoan everything."

"But she has to be like a lady. In order to survive in this world she must. Or else she will be a laughingstock in society. God, woman, what do I know of that — or her mother for that matter. It is you who can train her. You can show her what she must do."

Gently Mrs King placed one finger under his grizzled chin and made him look her in the eye. "Think, Obie, she is so like you. Where would she have gone if she couldn't find you when she went down to the old village? What would make her take off so?"

Obadiah shrugged his shoulders and let out a long sigh. "She came to look for me, you say? Well, I went to the inn. She wouldn't dare step foot inside it, or I would have her locked in Beckton Abbey for a month! No, there was no one by the boats; the only person I saw was… Oh, no, she could have been listening... If that was the case then she may have acted foolishly yet again." He turned to storm back out.

"What is it, Obie?" Mrs King interrupted.

"Arnold came to me at the back of the inn. He brought news of the trouble, trouble that could involve Daniel Tranton. But why would she act on that? She has no connection to the man, yet." He shrugged his shoulders, clearly bemused.

"Because they have met and they seem to like each other." Mrs King watched his eyes widen. "It was when she went on one of her ventures into the gill, she met him with an injured boy. It is something she wanted to talk to you about, but she could not find you."

"And that daughter of mine, always hanging out on the Hamiltons' land helped him, somehow, didn't she?"

She nodded.

"By all that's sacred I swear I will sort that lass out. She will be wed before winter comes, if her reputation does not already lie in ruins. I'll have to take a nag from the inn and ride over the moor road. Damnation, a son could not have been more hard work!"

Ivy had dressed Gladys in her day coat and hat and sat her down in the hallway near the front door while she found a coat that was more befitting of a lady's companion from Gladys' older outfits.

"Right, love, let's preamble!" she said.

Gladys looked her old friend in the eye, easy as they were of a height and similar build. "It's 'promenade' … we are going to promenade along the lower cliff path and take the air, Ivy."

"Aye, well you take the air wherever you want! I've had years of it blasting me lungs out. No, lass, we'll walk a ways and chat and be seen. Then you can tell me what words I'm supposed to use for when we meet posh folk. But in the meantime we'll figure out what to do with that man of yours." Ivy opened the door and they stepped outside. Gladys almost shrank back inside the house, but Ivy had a firm hold on her. "No, you don't, we're going to get you up and moving again. Why should he have a life while you merely exist?"

Gladys put her head up and fixed a smile on her face as they crossed the newly laid road that ran along the lower cliff. They walked for about twenty minutes and then took a seat on a small bench that overlooked the river mouth.

Ivy looked over her shoulder and saw Obadiah leaving the hotel.

"Glad, sit here a while, I forgot … something, back in a minute." She patted Gladys on her shoulder and crossed back over to the hotel.

Obadiah turned, and saw Gladys crossing the road in one of her new coats, one of her many. God, the woman would look like a sack of coal in anything, he thought, as he squinted against the light. But as the spectre took form in front of him he realised it was not his 'beloved' wife, but Ivy.

"Been getting gifts off her, Ivy. It suits you better." He forced a half smile onto his lips but his mind was elsewhere. He needed to find his daughter. Why were women so bloody difficult, he wondered?

"Obadiah Pennington, should we talk here or step inside?" She nodded to the hotel.

He tilted his head up and looked at her. Now what? he wondered.

"Ivy, I've got to go, I have business… Is that Gladys sat out there in the open?" He could hardly believe his eyes. She had not left the house for weeks.

"Aye, so why don't you go and say hello to your wife, Obadiah." Ivy looked at him and then glanced up at the hotel.

"I'm busy." He turned away from her.

"There was a time you would never have turned away from me, Obie. What was it you used to say, 'Ivy, you wrap yourself around me and I'll always be your steadfast oak'?"

He put his tongue in his cheek and looked down momentarily whilst he thought about his reply. "That was a long time past and…"

"And you were a young bastard then and now you are probing yourself to be an even bigger old one now!"

"No, lass, you married another."

"Yes, because you would not," she said, and stepped forward so that she was right in front of him.

"I was too young," he said and shook his head. "Why this, why now of all times?"

"I married him because I needed a man and I needed a father for the child you had put in my belly."

Obadiah took a step backwards. "You lie!"

"No, Obie, I may be many things but a liar I am not. My man knew I had fallen, but unlike you he loved me. More than that he had never had a child from his first marriage. She died childless and he thought it was him not her. So he took our Annie as our own. And I'd claw your eyes out before I'd give her up to you after seeing what you've done to that lass, Laura. But does the princess in your castle really know what Obadiah Pennington is like, eh?" She nodded to the hotel behind her.

Obadiah cleared his throat. "What do you want then?" he asked. "Say it once because we won't be having this conversation again."

"You talk to your womenfolk. Give them their independence from you. Let them live in a place where they can hold their heads up high. You stay away unless they want you still, and give my man a raise and me a small dowry for Annie for when she does wed."

"You do not ask much, woman, do you?" he said. "I suppose you want me to give you and Annie places in this home my womenfolk are to share at my expense."

"No, Obie, I do not want to share a gilded cage, I want to breathe fresh air, see my grandchildren run on the beach and play free from all your fancy folk. I love my man and daughter, and my home. God, I wouldn't swap any of them for the mess you've made of yours. I tell you, Obie, you ought to look to the future because you are no longer that handsome young fisherman I fell for who could jump from beach to coble in one smooth move. Why don't you speak to Gladys, she is still your wife." She looked to where the woman sat staring out to sea.

"Why don't you. Say goodbye for me and don't ever seek to bargain with me again. I have only your word that the lass is from me, and you lifted your skirts easily enough as I recall." His fist was balled at his side.

"Yes, you only have my word and that is all you need because I have never played false. Think on my offer, Obie, for if not I will seek other ways, and you need the people of Ebton — your men and women who toil for you — to have a heart to do so. Good day, Obadiah!" she said, and crossed back over to Gladys.

Behind the open window at the corner of the ground floor of the hotel Mrs Myrtle King stood with her back against the wall listening to her man being put in his place. She now understood why she had been ignored by the fisherwoman; she had been uncovered as 'the mistress', ironically by one who he had already wooed and used; possibly his first conquest.

Ivy was right about Obadiah, but Myrtle knew she had the advantage because she held his heart in her hands along with his good will. He needed and wanted her, and who else was going to take him on and keep him happy as he aged? He already was showing the signs of his years of hard work. Strangely, when a man stopped toiling physically and began to have a softer life, it was then that the decline in health started. There was so much more stress involved in running his new ventures than overseeing a few fishing boats.

Annie was as wilful as Laura but not as bright. It would not do for the girl to get any ideas, so if Ivy thought it best that she should never know who her father was then all to the good. She would advise him to settle a sum on them and sign a paper to state they would make no further claim on him in the event that he died.

She glanced back down as Ivy walked across to Gladys Pennington again and Obadiah stormed off on his way. If he did not discuss it with her, then perhaps he was not so under her control as she had thought; in which case more persuasion would be needed to secure her own future.

Obadiah rode into Gorebeck as if the devil was burning a trail behind him. His temper was such that he could have set the town alight. He dismounted outside the inn, but there was no sign of Laura. Where had she got to?

He was about to ask around when he realised what a fool he had been. He only had to find where the horse was stabled and then he would track his daughter down. He walked his horse into the hotel stables and saw Misty, already unsaddled and settled in a stall. So whatever she was about it definitely involved staying here overnight. If she thought running away from home was an answer to any problem, then she had less sense than he gave her credit for.

Daniel knew that Roderick would have left the mill at this hour of the day so instead of seeking him in his office he headed straight for the house he owned, which was located in a separate part of town surrounded by a large dry-stone wall and apple orchard. The man had sense; he had no wish to breathe in his own manufactories' fumes. Fortunately for Gorebeck, the mill was slightly outside of the town itself on a bend of a river, surrounded by trees. It could hardly be compared with the large-scale mills that polluted towns and cities elsewhere, but Roderick distanced himself from the rabble that manned it.

Daniel rode up to the house, tied his horse's reins to the hook by the colonnade and walked up the four steps to the large black painted door. A brass lion head knocker stared back at him, but he ignored it and opened the door.

It was easy to work out where the man was because Daniel could smell the food. Roderick was just finishing his dinner when Daniel walked in, ignoring a protesting housekeeper who, on hearing the door slam shut, had emerged in a somewhat bothered state.

"You, again!" Roderick swallowed the last of his glass of wine, as if Daniel was going to rip it from his hands. "Do you always have to burst in as though the devil himself was after you?" He placed the empty glass back down on the table and glared at the flustered woman standing in the doorway of the dining room, unsure as to what to do.

Daniel turned, smiled at her and, as he moved to the doorway, she backed off. He closed the door behind him as Roderick waved the woman away.

"Out with it, what brings you here this time?" Roderick sat back in his chair and belched. Wiping his mouth on his linen napkin he tossed it carelessly down onto his cleared plate.

Daniel approached the end of the long table and stood to the side of his cousin whilst keeping an eye focused through the window on the main road into Gorebeck over the bridge. He looked at Roderick. "You must listen to me, Roderick, and take my words very seriously, for I am not teasing you this time," Daniel began. He noticed a rider in the distance, approaching the town at a pace.

"But you say nothing." Roderick coughed. "Port?" he offered Daniel, gesturing to a cut crystal bottle at the side of the table.

"No, thank you. You need to have a clear head so pause in your drinking for a while and listen to my words. It's about Bullman. I tell you he is as rotten as the contents of a cess pit…"

Roderick laughed. "Your education has let your words down again, Daniel. Breeding comes out in the end, though," he drawled. Daniel ignored his remark wondering if the man was half cut already. How much wine had he drunk?

Undeterred he continued, "Listen! He is trying to do us both harm! I have proof that he is cheating you of monies from the purchases and sales of goods. Believe me he has high ambition and seeks to run both the mills with his own men." Daniel glanced at the man slumped in his chair before him, who seemed completely unperturbed about this revelation. "Do you not hear me…? He would do us harm!" Daniel stressed the words again, slower this time in case he had not taken his meaning in. Still there was no shock or reaction from his cousin. Something was wrong.

"Must I listen to you, Daniel?" Roderick looked up at Daniel, who, glancing back out at the approaching rider, saw that it was Mr Obadiah Pennington. What was he doing here? He blinked and looked back down at Roderick.

"Yes!"

"So, what do you want me to do? Sack him, or have him arrested as a swindler, or wait until he strikes and have him hanged for hiring men to take you down?"

Daniel's head that had drifted back to the window spun around as he saw the smug expression on Roderick's face. A horrid realisation dawned upon him. "You knew all along?" Anger was sweeping through his body, replacing the previous deep concern. What could this mean? Surely not that he was complicit with their plans, not his own cousin?

"Ah, you think me so stupid. That is your downfall, Daniel, your utter arrogance. What is it called, a soldier's intuition?" Roderick laughed, placing both stubby hands on the table and levering himself around, scraping the chair against the dark wood of the polished hemlock flooring. "Tell me, though, cousin," he sneered, "Who is it that spends his time looking to ledgers to make sense of the numbers? Who is it who has seen his profits dwindle in the last year or so? Me! That's who. So you think that I have no knowledge of what is happening to my own mill?" He was grinning wide, enjoying his moment, but Daniel was not. He was confused. If Roderick knew all this then why had he not come to Daniel for help?

"You know all this and did not tell me? You are telling me that you knew about his men, the ones he brought in to do me harm and you never said a word. Are you in on this, Roderick?" Daniel clenched his fists at his side to stifle the overwhelming emotions that tore at his heart. He had never been close to Roderick; admittedly, he had enjoyed bettering him in sport, cards and with the fairer sex, but he had never thought that the man would partake in Daniel's downfall ... plan a murder.

"No, Daniel. I would not break the law and risk everything my father worked for just to spite you.... Although it was tempting, you have cut me to the core over the years, Daniel. You were blessed with good looks and I not so and you used this against me time and time again, instead of offering a hand of friendship. What a good cousin you are!"

Daniel felt a rare pang of guilt, a very unusual feeling where Roderick was concerned, but he held the man's focus and said nothing. He did not come here to apologise for his past failings of vanity but to save his mill, and his life.

"Let me explain. You see, Hamilton, my father-in-law to be..." Roderick smiled as he paused to see Daniel's curious expression. "Hamilton knew Bullman from before the wars. He recognised him on a trip to town last year. At the time I was beginning to realise what I had inadvertently taken on as a foreman, and was lost as to how to deal with the man. Hamilton saw him and left straight away before Bullman could see him. The following day I was asked to visit him, privately. I was flattered, of course, as it offered the chance to dine with both he and the delightful Sarah Hamilton. A fairer young maid you will not see this side of Harrogate. He told me that Bullman was a hardened soldier, who took the King's shilling three times over, deserted twice and was disbanded once, ran away to avoid a life in gaol. He had been a troublemaker, but it was Hamilton who had him arrested back then and the man swore he would seek his revenge if ever they crossed paths again. He escaped, as he seemed to have an aptitude at doing that. He actually swam from the hulks on the Thames. I am surprised the water did not poison him. You have to admire the man's ability to survive." Roderick paused and poured himself another wine but Daniel moved the glass beyond his reach.

"Continue," he said simply. "So what is all this to do with me?"

"Nothing, I have been working with Captain Gillick at the barracks. We have given the man enough slack to hang himself and can put his ruffians away for good. He wants to catch the three that were loitering on the road for you. You see you have been watched."

"Not always," Daniel said. "I could have been killed only today."

"Oh, yes you were, just as you were a few days since, for who else but a notable man of the country such as Arnold Glynn could send a hunt in the wrong direction, instead of leading them straight to a fool who should not be muddying his boots to save an urchin like Jebediah Flitch." Roderick heard the loud knock on the door and shouted to the housekeeper. "Damnation, who is it now!"

"Mr Obadiah Pennington, arriving at speed," Daniel replied.

"Let him in," Roderick ordered.

The door opened and Pennington blustered in. He stared at Daniel and then looked to Roderick. "My daughter, she…"

"Your daughter is in the hotel, safe," Daniel answered. "No harm has or will come to her, I promise you that, Obadiah." He ignored the chortle in Roderick's throat. Daniel had the urge to grip it more and more and yet that had been his problem, hadn't it? He was always willing to slap Roderick down, without realising it had been so. For a split second he was engulfed by a feeling of shame as he thought himself to be a better person. Perhaps before the wars he had not been so.

"She heard Arnold talking to me about Bullman's heavies. She had no way of knowing that I was waiting for the militia to take their places." Obadiah glanced up at the now flushed face of Daniel Tranton.

Roderick stood up and laughed. Daniel could not remember when he had seen him look so animated and happy. For the first time he realised it was his own jealousy that had barred their friendship, for Roderick had the love of a good mother when he was a child and Daniel had one who would use him as a trinket, an adornment to be discussed at her soirees. "I have the militia about to descend on the Hare and Rabbit where they are all meeting in the tap room. They will be rounded up. I'll have my money back in my bank, and I'll announce my marriage to the beautiful Miss Sarah Hamilton in the coming month, as her father is so very grateful to me for removing the shadow that has been cast over his life since that fateful day when he saw Bullman in Gorebeck."

"But the militia were nowhere to be seen today when the three men were going to take me down," Daniel began.

"Ah, well, they were not to do that until Monday."

Daniel leaned over the table at Roderick. "If not for the bravery of a young maid I would have been kidnapped or dead!" Daniel spat his words out.

Roderick waved a hand away dismissively. "Nonsense, it was a momentary oversight. They would have all hanged. So, gentlemen, if you will excuse me, I will bid you good day, the housekeeper will show you out. Feel free to have a drink before you leave." Roderick strode purposefully out of the room.

Obadiah looked at Daniel. "Sorry, lad! I was ordered not to tell you." He then drank down a glass of wine in one swift gulp.

Daniel smiled back at him. "What madness has surrounded me for months and I had no notion it was happening."

"You see, you always wanted to better Roderick…" Obadiah cleared his throat. "So they thought that it was better if things ran their course. They did not want to put them away for a short time, they wanted Bullman to hang."

"And your letter, your offer, was that somehow linked into this plan of yours?" Daniel asked.

"No, lad, but I thought that if I made it sound as if you were in competition with your cousin for Laura's hand and the trade links, then you'd take an interest. She's a good girl, Daniel." Obadiah looked at him through sad, tired eyes.

"You know me so well, Obadiah. Better than I do myself it seems." Daniel sighed. "I was a bit of a headstrong ass before I went to war it appears."

"Only a bit of one." Obadiah smiled. "I'm sorry, lad, if you got into danger. I thought they had your back covered."

"Don't be."

"Do you not feel put out?" Obadiah asked. He gestured towards the doorway through which Roderick had flounced out.

"No, not really, let him have his moment of pride. I've had my share over the years at his expense, but he will regret the day he marries that empty-headed, fickle girl, Miss Sarah Hamilton. She'll cost him a fortune. Roderick will suffer, just as his wallet will."

Obadiah laughed. "Oh, do not talk to me about regretting marriage or the tribulations suffered at the hands of women. I'd better see to my daughter. We have things to settle between us."

Daniel nodded. "May I come? I would like to make good on your offer, if she is open to it. I would not consider marrying just to spite my cousin."

Obadiah sighed. "She is angry with me, Daniel. I think I may have lost her trust, so she will need a good man, a reliable one to replace me for I have fallen short of her expectations, as her mother did of mine. She knows about my mistress, Mrs King, and she does not understand."

The housekeeper opened the door but stayed outside of the room.

"I think you underestimate her," Daniel said, as they left the house.

Obadiah looked shocked. "That is the second time today I have been told I do not know my own girl!"

"Then that is at the heart of it, for she is a girl no longer," Daniel remarked.

Chapter 10

Three women sat in Mrs King's small parlour, sipping tea and waiting for her maid to leave them alone. Once the door was closed Mrs King took her seat again by the fire. Opposite her was Mrs Gladys Pennington and her 'companion'.

"To what do I owe this pleasure, Mrs Pennington?" Mrs King opened the conversation to break the tension that filled the air. She calmly ignored Ivy as the woman had her earlier. It gave her the faintest feeling of pleasure that she now had the opportunity to return the favour.

Gladys pointed to the footstool set slightly aside from her chair in the small room, and said, "Ivy, set yourself down on that."

Ivy tugged the stool to the side of her new mistress's chair and hunkered down on it.

"This visit is well overdue, Mrs King. I want to know how the hotel does," Gladys said.

The fresh sea air, or something, seemed to have perked the old bat up, Mrs King thought. "How the hotel does … what?" she asked, as if she had no idea at all what the woman referred to. The fact was that, as a hotel, it would have been closed down at least three months since, as at most she had one long term retired gentleman and the occasional guest who stayed a night or two; but Obadiah did not care, for as long as she was there he had what he wanted.

"I have not noticed many guests passing by, so I wondered how the hotel did?" Gladys repeated.

"Perhaps it is because you do not sit by the window and look out often enough."

Gladys held her icy stare. Mrs King could feel the force of the anger simmering within Gladys, which she would never have credited possible from the weak-minded female that her husband so often described to her.

"That is true…" Gladys replied, "but I have never been one for gossip and you never know what idle tittle-tattle can start from people observing the comings and goings of others. Sometimes even your closest friends and neighbours can cause unwanted pain." The stare continued.

Mrs King broke eye contact first. She glanced at Ivy's smug face and realised these women were on a mission of confrontation, but what did they really want? Could they seriously think she would run away, shame-faced, and leave Obadiah?

"Your point being, Mrs Pennington?" she asked, chin held high.

"That if your hotel is failing — sorry, I meant my husband's hotel is failing — then perhaps you need some help to make it a greater success." Gladys tilted her head slightly, but the expression and the ice in the eyes remained unchanged.

"I manage the hotel impeccably. I can assure you that every room is clean and the food is hearty and…" Mrs King found her confident words faltering.

"Oh, you misunderstand my meaning, I do not doubt that you control everything within these walls in a proficient manner, but still you are in need of more customers, are you not? I would hate to see all your efforts go to waste." The woman's lips turned up at the corner but a smile did not break across the mouth and certainly did not reach her eyes.

"Then what is it you are proposing, Mrs Pennington, because I admit to being slightly confused by this visit and fail to understand your intentions?"

"It is simply this, Mrs King. My husband, who you know so well," there was a slight pause in her words and despite her best intentions Mrs King felt her cheeks colour slightly, "has an eye for a good investment. His ambition and desires know no end, but in this establishment his business sense is lacking. I would suggest that you need people of a certain class directed here. In this, I believe, I have a solution."

"Do tell me what you are proposing, for I am all attention," Mrs King said, but made no stance regarding the defence of her situation with Obadiah that his wife had clearly hinted at.

"You run the hotel. I am expecting my Laura, my daughter, to become engaged in the not so distant future. We will need to travel to Harrogate, York or beyond to find her a suitable dress. Whilst there, we will take the waters, visit spas and mix with the new money, like ourselves. Those who aspire to greater things than our birthright entailed. I intend to spread the word of the health-giving qualities of taking to the waters at 'Ebton by the Sea'. I shall venture to Brighton if need be, on the south coast, and see if they have salt treatments, or have used seaweed for skin cure, cold baths for those with malaise. We shall have cards printed and I shall leave them wherever I go and stay. Word will get around and your business should begin to thrive. Of course, I shall write to you and state my findings and if I need a room preparing for such treatments."

Mrs King was completely taken aback. "Why would you do this for the hotel, for Ebton?" she asked, and then added, "Does Mr Pennington know of your plans?"

"Because I want to see Obadiah's wealth increase, as he would too. I want to see this hotel beget sister hotels along the bay, because I too have ambition and wish to be a part of the bay's exciting new developments."

Mrs King could see that the woman did have a strong passion, but it had been buried deep for far too long. Poor Gladys, she thought.

"I want, and would need, a good allowance for myself and Laura, and I will need my own carriage to take us around." At this point the hard-steely stare from Gladys Pennington's eyes mellowed to one that showed her absolute joy at the idea of travelling the region in her own carriage with her daughter. Then Mrs King understood.

"So you would leave Ebton?" Mrs King asked. "And your husband?"

"Temporarily, yes," Gladys replied. "I will leave Ebton but my husband I will never truly leave because we are married for better or worse. Just because it has turned out the latter case does not mean I will not work to improve our lot here. I am married and that cannot and will not change. I may not physically have or hold him but we were wed before God and till death we shall not part!"

"That is very noble and loyal of you. I would expect nothing less from someone who has been married so long." Mrs King smiled and saw that her reaction had surprised her lover's wife, for the one thing she had never considered was that the respectable widow preferred to be just that and no man's wife, not anymore. "And you would be taking Ivy with you as your companion?" Mrs King asked.

"No!" Ivy, startled at the suggestion, obviously appalled at the idea. "My home, my life and my man are all here." She looked to Gladys, obviously concerned. "Why would I leave them? I don't want to go traipsing around foreign parts in no carriage, I'd feel right sick."

"No, Ivy will stay here and look after the house with Annie. I shall return at times and will need my home kept ready.

Besides, someone needs to keep an eye on the place. However, I will be speaking to my husband when he returns. I am sure he will agree and that absence, in our case at least, can only make the heart grow fonder. He will be in good hands, I am sure, as he has so many loyal friends around him to do his bidding." She smiled at Mrs King, who nodded knowingly back. "Very well, it seems our business here is done. In future we shall talk of hotel matters if necessary and of nothing else."

"Good day, Mrs Pennington," Mrs King said and stood back so both of her visitors could pass her by.

"Good day, Mrs King," Gladys Pennington said and strode out with her head held high.

The drinkers at the Hare and Rabbit were taken by surprise when a commotion broke out as the militia burst in and shouted out the names of the men they had come for: starting with Ivor Bullman.

He made a break for the back doorway and would have had a chance of getting away but for the serving wench, May, who stepped into his pathway causing both of them to fall to the ground. It cost her a slap on the face from Bullman's hand as he rose, but that was nothing to the pain that shot through his skull when a rifle butt contacted it with force.

Six men, including the three that had tried to waylay Daniel, were propelled out into the street. Rarely had the town seen such a sight. Ivor Bullman was dragged out last and clamped in irons before being thrown into the back of a drab wagon. The population of Gorebeck came out of their houses and shops to stare as Ivor Bullman and his men were arrested. The six men were given a choice on the spot of marching off with the King's shilling in their pocket, except Bullman, who was taken away straight back to the hulks he escaped from by order of the magistrates; the rest could always choose to languish until their cases could be heard in York assizes. They marched.

Laura watched the men approach, it was her father and Mr Tranton … Daniel, who walked toward the hotel. She decided to take a seat at the side of the small lounge and await their arrival, rather than be found staring out at the spectacle. Besides, if she was in a public area of the building her father was less likely to explode at her most recent adventure.

They entered the hotel's small lobby. Her father's eyes found her straightaway. She felt anxious but did not give into a desire to smile; they had gone beyond that point. She swallowed as they walked over to her, pulling two chairs with them so they could sit by her. A vision of a bird trapped in a cage came into her head.

"Laura…" her father began to speak.

"Father. Mr Tranton, I am glad that you both look to be safe and well." She forced a smile and looked from one to the other. Her cheeks felt warm and she hoped she had not coloured too deeply.

"Laura," her father continued, ignoring her comments. "What am I to do with you? I have built a small fortune to settle upon your future, my legacy to you and your children, when you have them, and yet you are still so reckless!" he said in a calm, strangely controlled manner.

"Well, I thought…" She looked at Daniel who seemed to be almost biting his lip to hold back his words.

"Yes, exactly, Laura, you thought, you acted and you did not see fit to ask me, child. Did it not cross your mind that I may know more of the matter than what your overzealous ears heard whilst you lurked in the shadows of an inn, like a…"

"Do you not think that I tried? You were otherwise 'engaged'?"

To her surprise, instead of responding to her he spoke to Daniel. "I have let the girl down and now she is a wilful woman. Do you think you can become engaged to such a lady and still make a good marriage?" Obadiah's words sounded as tired as his face looked.

Daniel smiled, but Laura snapped, "I will not be discussed in such a manner as if I am not here, Father! I may have acted rashly, but in a good cause. You were going to leave Daniel, and men were trying to hurt him. I saved him from them!"

Obadiah chuckled. "Did she?" he asked.

"Yes, in a way she did. I may have been watched by Roderick's soldiers, but there was a very strong chance the men could have acted before anyone could have stopped them. It would appear that fate has brought Laura and I together. If it is with both your approval, I would like to walk out with her…" Daniel paused, turning to Laura, "I would like to consider an engagement between us. We, it seems, both have a tendency to act rashly, and I think if I have learned nothing else from this whole experience it is that perhaps I cannot do everything in life on my own."

Obadiah stood up. "Laura, you have my blessing to be with this man and to consider your future. We must return, though, and leave him to sort out the mess here, whilst we sort out the mess that I left at home. We will talk on the ride back."

"Very well," Laura said, as obediently as she could, but her eyes and Daniel's were fixed upon each other's.

"Daniel, when you've done here and after the meeting, perhaps you could visit and let me know your decision then."

"Certainly, Obadiah." Daniel smiled at Laura.

"But, Laura, you will need to learn to behave properly and…" Obadiah began to say.

"No threats, Father. I will not let you down, I am too old for school, but it seems I still have a lot to learn."

"Yes, we both do. But on our return you will speak earnestly with your mother because changes have to be made and I have put them off for too long." Obadiah wiped his tired eyes. He was obviously not relishing the meeting. Obadiah nodded to Daniel and walked away, leaving Laura to follow in his wake.

Laura hesitated. "Mr Tranton…"

"Daniel, please." He smiled.

"Daniel, I would like us to become better acquainted. Could I come and stay near your mill, in Beckton, and with my mother as my chaperone? I think that a change of air would benefit her and we could go to Harrogate easily from there and take the waters. She would like that. I can in time know the man you are and the life you live, and you can become acquainted with my bothersome nature."

"Yes. I think that would be an excellent idea. I can explain my desire to create a future where a mill cares for its workers and you can see the small community that I am nurturing."

"Yes," she said excitedly.

"Laura!" her father snapped back at her and, so to avoid anyone looking at them further, she went to the mounting block and took her seat on Misty again.

Father and daughter rode in silence at first and at a canter. Once the moor was crossed and the sea was in sight they slowed as they made their way down the long bank that would lead to the coastal plain. When Ebton was just visible, nestled before the three-hundred-foot-high headland of Stangcliffe, Obadiah slowed his horse to a standstill and waited for Laura to ride alongside.

"It is beautiful," she remarked, to break the awkward silence that filled the air between them.

"Don't hate me, Laura," he said quietly, and his voice almost broke. His eyes stared at the expanse before them.

Laura could not remember a time when he had ever spoken in such a way to her. She looked at him and wondered why she had never noticed how grizzled his hair was now and how many of the creases in his skin lined his eyes.

"How could I hate you when you are my father?" she asked, realising that the love she had held for him for so long far outweighed any newer feelings of hatred. Yet, disappointment gnawed away at it and dulled it. Perhaps, she wondered, the fault had lain with her. Did she expect too much of him? No, he was a grown man and old enough to take the blame for what he had done to his family. "But I don't like what you've done to Ma," she said as they walked their horses along side by side.

"What do you mean, what I've done to her?" His voice rose. He obviously found the notion incredulous. "You have no idea of what I have had to put up with over the years. She has neglected her husband and sorely used me as a result."

"What can a woman do within a marriage to neglect their husband? You've trapped her in the very lifestyle that she dreamed of having, but instead of giving her joy it has become as a cocoon that threatens to suffocate her. Her neighbour is her husband's lover and has been for some considerable time, her old friends think that she is a cut above them now, and she does not ride and therefore cannot escape. So, unless she hides away, or has a carriage to take her beyond Ebton, how is she to socialise at all?"

Obadiah was obviously taken aback, yet defensive. "My God, you are a direct one, aren't you?" he said. "Daniel will have to sort that out."

"Father, don't prevaricate. If I decide to consider Mr Daniel Tranton as a prospective husband then he will have to be man enough to accept a woman with a mind and will of her own. If he does not, then I will not let any man trap me in such a fashion. I would rather live and die alone." She stared ahead of her, determined not to let him undermine the resolve she had fostered, as he had done so often in her life.

"Oh, what nonsense! What of my legacy to you and future generations? The name of Pennington will linger in the town if it cannot directly be passed from mother to son. What of everything I have built up here, if you don't have a child, what will it all have been for?"

"If I had a boy child, a grandson for you, you mean, unlike the useless daughter that you sired!" she challenged him.

"Yes, a boy! Because that is how the world is, lass, and no amount of whinging about it will ever change it. Men are stronger and women fairer, that is as nature intended so don't you get uppity with me! I can do a lot for you but change the natural order of life is not within my power, so respect your place in the way of things and stop bemoaning it."

They were silent whilst they traversed a rugged piece of the road.

"You really think your mother is trapped and not just angry?" he asked, quite sheepishly.

"Yes." Laura looked at him, but he turned away. "And angry too," she added. "Perhaps neither of you lived up to the other's expectations. That is a travesty, don't you think, for you both sought to have more than you were given in life? If only you could have worked together..." She let her voice trail off on the breeze.

"If only! They are two very simple words to say. I knew Myrtle first and we loved each other long before I knew your ma. I thought Myrtle was the prettiest, most lovely creature I had ever set my eyes upon, but I was never good enough for her father, until it was too late."

"Creature! She was a young woman, not an animal to own. Perhaps you once loved each other in a time before you had the bond of marriage to separate you. You are married, Pa, and you took up with her again. Did those vows not mean anything to you?"

"You wouldn't understand," he said, his voice low, eyes downcast.

"Give me a chance to then?" Laura prompted. He steadied his horse.

"Very well, if you think you are so worldly, then I will tell you. She stopped doing what a wife should do for her husband as her womanly duty, and so how was I supposed to carry on as if all was well when it wasn't, and I'm not saying anymore on the subject than that. It became obvious that I would never have a son."

"Why?" Laura asked.

"That is hardly the issue! You miss the point, she is my wife, she should just ... do...!" His face reddened further. "We should not talk of this. Even in the most base places this is not a discussion a father and daughter should ever have."

Laura hoped that he would not have a failure of the heart, but there were things that needed saying.

"Perhaps not, but don't you realise that the fact you did not ask may well have compounded things? You had no interest in why she 'went off her duties' and that must surely have worsened the problem. There could have been good reason. You could have asked and not demanded…" Laura saw his mouth set in a firm line.

"I never demanded. I am not an animal, girl. Is that what you think of me?" He looked genuinely hurt.

"Well … or sulked," she added.

"Aye, well that's as maybe, but I am a man and a man has needs a wife should … accommodate." He coughed and wiped his forehead with his hand.

"So you found your 'accommodation' at the hotel instead and that's the end of it is it? You were satisfied, and your wife was trapped!" Laura stated, proving in her own mind at least that her assumption was correct.

"You make it sound so simple. When you are wed you will have some understanding of what we talk about. As it is, your words are full of ignorance and innocence, so I forgive you. I will not give up my 'accommodation' and I will be telling your mother so on our return. I will speak with her first, then you can come in and pacify her and talk to her of Mr Daniel Tranton. She will look forward to his visit at least and the prospect of a wedding to plan and fuss over, but it will be a Beckton and not an Ebton wedding. You will see that your mama is very keen to see you suitably 'trapped' too." He did not try to disguise the bitter sarcasm in his voice.

"Father, do you not even want to listen to what she has to say about your revelation to her? You are going to tell her and walk away and leave me to deal with her distress! You could break her heart, Pa, as well as mine." Laura loved him but was struggling to not tell him that he was being totally selfish.

"My dear girl, I have lived with your mother long enough to know that she will not say ought to me. She will cry, weep, wail and sip that blasted tincture that sends her into oblivion and then she will turn for you to come and comfort her so that you will feel even more pity for her and lessen your love for me. You must be strong, Laura, and prop her up. Make her behave well and let her be respectable for Daniel so that we can see about your wedding. I cannot abide living this lie anymore and I will not be controlled by her fits and fancies…"

"Father, breathe before your heart bursts."

"Oh, well, why not let it, seeing as I have broken yours already," he snapped.

Laura looked at him. She did not know which one she felt the most pity for; her ma perhaps, because at least he was having fun and a life worth living with a woman who wanted and understood him, and what did her ma have? The answer that resounded in her mind was — her!

"You will have Daniel Tranton in your life who will replace the need of a father and then you will understand the difference between a happy marriage and an empty one."

She loved her father dearly, but what surprised her was the realisation that this man who had seen how to transform a whole bay was as blinkered as a horse on a track. He had no empathy for his wife or daughter at all. For the first time Laura wondered what on earth her mother ever saw in him, other than a way out of the poverty she had been born into. An overwhelming sadness threatened to sweep through her for she realised that these two people could have been so right for each other if not for the presence of a very attractive and educated woman called Mrs Myrtle King.

Chapter 11

Roderick Tranton had sent word directly to Mr Hamilton at his estate as soon as Bullman had been arrested, and eagerly awaited the invitation to attend him at his earliest convenience. To his chagrin the reply did not come by return and annoyingly he had to spend time reorganising his workers to fill the gap that Bullman and his men left. This he allowed Daniel Tranton and the man Sleights a hand in to speed things up.

Roderick had done his country a great service and allowed his mill to be used to catch a man who had been wanted for some time, so now he would claim his reward. At last, he would be a married man to a wife that would make him the envy of the region. Daniel Tranton could find himself some mill worker if he wanted one — he would not have Sarah Hamilton.

Roderick's moment of self-satisfaction ended abruptly when a hullabaloo ripped through the courtyard, like the death cry of a banshee, right in front of his office.

"Mr Tranton! Mr Tranton! Please stop them, they're threatening to turn me out of me hearth and home!" Mrs Cookson's shrill voice exploded into the air as she ran across from the schoolroom, skidding on the damp cobbled stones near to where he stood.

"What is the meaning of this, Daniel?" Roderick shouted across to his cousin as he appeared in the schoolroom doorway.

"She is the common law wife to one of Bullman's men. She has no hearth and home here and has been taking a share of the money given her for wax tablets, books and chalk." Daniel folded his arms and waited for Roderick to reply.

"Get gone, woman, and be grateful you have not been sent to the York assizes with Ivor Bullman," Roderick said as she grasped his sleeve.

Mrs Cookson cursed and spat as she stepped back. "You'll die o' the pox, the lot of yer!" she growled.

"And if you don't hush that vile mouth of yours I will see you burnt as a witch!" Roderick jabbed his finger into her shoulder. "Get ye gone!"

She backed away and skulked towards the gate. "You're all damned," she cursed as she went.

Roderick saw red. "Take her to the lockup, Sleights. If she hasn't calmed that tongue of hers by morning she can go to the assizes with her man!"

Stunned and now whimpering incoherently, the woman was frogmarched along the cobbled street beyond the gates.

"Mr Tranton! Mr Tranton!" A rider arrived holding a letter in his hand.

"What now?" Roderick said, then realised that this was what he had been waiting for.

Daniel wandered over to his cousin.

"Now, my dear Daniel," Roderick said proudly. "This is my betrothed's writing See, the girl cannot wait to meet me and thank me for helping her father rid himself of the bane of his life!" He eagerly ripped open the waxed seal.

Daniel waited for him to continue, but instead of further congeniality the man froze. Still holding the note in his hand, he remained almost motionless, if not for a slight tremble of the hand. Daniel wondered if he had had some kind of fit.

"Roderick? Speak to me, man." Daniel slipped the paper from the man's fingers and led him to the side of the buildings, away from the view of prying eyes. "What is it, Roderick? Tell me what has befallen you." But Roderick just stared beyond the gates at the distant figure of Mrs Cookson.

"I really am cursed," he said.

"What nonsense, man! How so?"

Roderick handed him the letter.

My dear Mr Tranton,

I am writing to thank you on behalf of my father and myself for the invaluable help that you have given us and the many mill owners who have suffered at the hands of Mr Ivor Bullman and his kind. We are eternally grateful to you.

Father and I will now be able to return to our mills in West Yorkshire where our fortune and family are preserved.

We hope that you will visit when you next can leave your small mill and perhaps enjoy a visit around one of the country's largest and most successful ones.

My father would have written himself, but we are at present in the process of announcing my engagement to Sir Gregory Hingston of Bristol. Their family and ours go back generations and I hope that you understand and find it in your heart to wish me much happiness...

Daniel put a hand on his cousin's shoulder, as the man fell back against the wall.

"Have your last laugh, young Daniel, for I will never make such a fool of myself again," Roderick said.

"No, Roderick, you will not. You will hold your head up high. That madam would have bled you dry and that I would have hated to see." Daniel rubbed Roderick's shoulder, trying to impress his words and their sincere meaning upon him.

"Would you really?" Roderick asked. He looked surprised.

"Sincerely. Please forgive me my arrogance of the past and I shall forgive you yours, the way you have treated people in your employ. Your mill and mine could work together, in tandem, to challenge some of the larger ones to the west. We live in a time of change, but if we adopt a method of work that acknowledges people's basic rights, their needs, then you can still have profit and there will be no grounds for the Luddites to cause a fuss."

"You really think that they would not want more and more until they bleed us dry?" Roderick asked

"There has to be lines drawn, but would you really have them live in dirty flea-ridden hovels like they do in Manchester, the pride of the new industry? Or instead have them healthy and doing a sound day's work and turning out cloth you can be proud of?"

"Very well! We will try it your way, but if trouble persists I will bring in the Yeomanry again."

"We have a deal cousin, so come and have a drink with me and send that flighty young wench a brief note wishing her well with good grace."

Roderick sighed and together they headed back towards the town and entered the inn.

It was a subdued father and daughter who entered Ebton. They took the horses around to the back of the terraces where the empty stable stalls were.

"Do you wish me there whilst you deliver your impending words of doom, Father?" Laura asked as she dismounted gracefully onto the mounting block.

Her father puffed as he swung his leg over the back of his saddle before landing heavily on his feet. "Your presence might soften the blow," he said.

"Can you not stand and deliver your words without me there? Can you not be that man, Father, who has the courage of his conviction? I will wait outside and enter when you leave, but this is one conversation you must have with your wife and face alone."

She stormed into the house with a reluctant Obadiah following in her wake.

Obadiah entered the morning room where Gladys was reading by the window seat. He had thought she would be dozing in her chair by the fire as she had the habit of, but Ivy was seated there, sewing something. He had entered to talk to his wife about living with his current mistress and there, bold as brass, in his own house was his first mistress! This was not at all what he had expected.

"You return, my husband." A calm voice greeted him. He paused, waiting for the remonstration, questions, accusations or demands. None came.

Obadiah looked into his wife's clear eyes. Her hair was washed and dressed, her attire brighter in hue than her normal day wear and her shoulders more upright.

"Ivy, leave us," Obadiah said. His eyes never left those of his composed wife. Had she been waiting for him? he wondered.

The woman smiled smugly at him but looked to Gladys for her permission to go. Ivy left, but the door was slightly ajar.

"Gladys, I have returned, but there is something I must tell you and I think you had better sit by the fire whilst I do so." He stood with his feet planted firmly on the ground and watched as she meekly did as he bid. Once she was seated and looking up at him, he continued. "The matter is simple and is not open for negotiation. The fact is that I have no wish to continue living with you as man and wife. You fail to provide any attempt at making me welcome in this home and I have, quite frankly, had enough." He stopped and stared at the woman before him, who sat straight-backed, hands nestled in her lap, whilst showing no emotion and still watching him.

"Did you not hear what I said to you, woman?" he asked.

"Yes, Obadiah, I did. My name is Gladys. You may remember that there was a time when you called me your 'Happy Glad'." She smiled up at him and he felt slightly wrong-footed for he did remember those days, but they were in the distant past.

"Well that was back then, and this is now, but you stopped being my 'Happy Glad', didn't you?" he said.

"Yes, why was that do you think?" she asked.

"If you are going to blame me for being hard at my work, carving out this home and making something of the area, then I will not take that!" he said, his voice rising.

"No, Obadiah, it was not because of that. It was because after the birth I found it difficult." Her calm answer struck at him harder than a tantrum of pleas would.

"Difficult? You had Ivy and the other women around you. My God, woman, do you expect everything in life to be easy?"

"Sit down, Obadiah, and talk to me properly, like you did once upon a time." She gestured to the chair opposite her at the other side of the marble hearth.

"I cannot, I have said my piece and I have to go to…" His voice drifted off as he glanced at the door behind him.

"To your lover? Is that why you cannot talk to your wife, because you cannot wait to fall into the arms of Mrs Myrtle King?"

Obadiah coloured. "You know. I suppose that daughter of ours could not wait to tell you after all."

"No, it was not Laura. I have known since you placed her so conveniently in your hotel. She is quite comely and pleasant, I suppose, if you like used goods. I think you will be well suited, but you will listen to me before you move there." She pointed to the chair.

"So you will divorce me?" he asked, eyes bright and hopeful for the first time in days.

"No, Obadiah, I will never divorce you, for we are wed for good or ill, but you may live with her as you like, whilst I stay in Beckton or Harrogate perhaps, with my Laura, until she is wed. Oh and to do what I plan, which is to encourage visitors to take the water treatments on offer at Ebton, we will require a coach."

"What water treatments?" he asked, wondering what on earth had happened to the dormouse of a wife who bored him to tears.

"The ones we shall have here. Mrs King will help to organise them."

"You have spoken of this plan to Myrtle?" He was incredulous.

"Of course! I need her here to run the things with the hotel," she explained.

"So you would make use of my…"

"Yes, for she is in your employ and besides that the hotel is not turning a profit. In fact, it runs at a loss, but it could be a small gold mine."

"You have thought this through carefully." Obadiah shook his head. Never underestimate a woman, he thought.

"Oh yes, I have had many hours to think on it."

"You would trade your husband for a coach and horse?" he said.

"Yes, for they would be far more use to me than you, Obadiah. Now to explain why I withdrew from our marriage bed; you see, I found it difficult to stomach a man making love to me and making eyes at another. I found that I had no appetite for it, and as for sharing you, well, that I was never going to do. You could make me ill, for if she would sleep with you, and ran a boarding house, then what was to stop her having the occasional fling for extra coin."

"How dare you infer…" His fists clenched at his side. He had never hit a woman, but Gladys was pushing him to his limit.

"How … dare . . I?" Gladys stood to her almost five feet in height and prodded her husband hard in the chest. It was her turn to look down into his startled eyes as he slumped into the fireside chair. "I dare because you have broken every promise you ever made to me! You promised I would have a coach of my own one day and by God I shall keep you to it. Your wench has been married before to a man who played around, and goodness only knows why she has never had a child, but, Obadiah, you can share what rot she carries with her, for I will not!"

Obadiah's breath became laboured. He had never felt such shock since the day he was told Myrtle King had wed another. "You have the tongue of a fisherwoman — that will not change, coach or no," he said.

"My words, my behaviour will change. I'll never be proper grand, Obadiah, but I will be adequately provided for. You see, I will bring business to Ebton for the people will come for the good of their health. I will have a share of your wealth and Laura will be married to a man who will cherish her. Not one who uses her and looks over his shoulder lusting after another!" She folded her arms across her chest and then when he did not instantly reply, walked towards the door.

"Have you no love for me left at all, Gladys?" Obadiah asked. He was cut to the core, for he had never considered that she would rejoice at being set free of him. She was supposed to weep and bemoan her fate. Suddenly it felt like it was he who was trapped. Her words had stung him. Obadiah stood up and tried to look proud, but the thought of his Myrtle with another man gnawed at his gut, whilst the image of his Gladys being 'Happy Glad' in her coach with Laura, traversing the countryside, left him feeling both empty and bereft. This had not gone well. It was supposed to be the moment he set himself free, so why did it feel the opposite? He would leave her now, and row out in his favourite coble with his men, and there on the seas, away from womenfolk, he would think.

She opened the door wide and, as he passed, simply said, "I will always have love for you, which is why I will never free you from our marriage. But you are half the man I thought you were when I married you, so I release you far enough to tell you to go to a woman who makes you feel whole with my consent."

Gladys turned her head away as he tried to peck her cheek. She would not even grant him that. Obadiah walked past Ivy and Laura who waited patiently outside and said nothing.

Chapter 12

The next two weeks flew past in a blur of activity in the Pennington household. Laura's mother was so involved in the arrangements for the arrival of her post chaise that she hardly stopped smiling. Her endless chatter and outings with her companion, Ivy, who was once more her best friend was reassuring, as together they learnt all they could about the mode of dress and the way of their 'betters'. Gladys had taken her daughter to Harrogate and back already. Designed for swift travel, the chaise could continue the journey from staging point to staging point.

Laura thought that her mother grew bolder each day and it filled her heart with joy to see it. For the past few years she had wondered what Obadiah had seen in his Gladys, but now she could see the subdued spirit that had been trapped within her was free again. Her wings began to spread a little further and the years seemed to roll back as her previously tired eyes now looked ahead and upwards rather than being forever downcast. It was as if the world was suddenly hers to explore.

When Daniel did not send word, Laura could not help feeling her own spirits were being stifled. Their time together had been short, yet intense and she had never felt so alive. But he had a mill, a future and the choice of many a fine lady of breeding. What need had he for a fisherman's daughter, whose father was unfaithful and whose mother was set to continue taking her around the county at her whim.

Laura even wondered if her father had somehow removed his offer of the marriage to spite her and her mother. After all, they had been so highhanded when he returned that he had seen his plan fall around his feet.

The evening before they set off to go and take the waters at Harrogate, Laura decided that she could not leave without seeing her father first. He may have been in the wrong as far as she was concerned but he was her father, her blood and she needed to find a place in her heart again for him to have that sense of peace she craved.

She made her way along the promenade and down the steep bank towards The Coble Inn. Mrs King had told her he was down there drinking … again.

"What brings you down here, Laura?" Annie's voice welcomed her as she left the shelter of the line of boats. "Don't tell me you miss me so dearly that you have come to see if I want to go a travelling with you as your very own companion?" Annie beamed at her, eyes shining in the fading light.

"I wish you would, Annie," Laura admitted. Since Annie had stopped working at the house she had sorely missed her. Ivy and Gladys ruled there; Laura could not get past Ivy as she had Annie.

"I wouldn't. I would feel like a court jester living amongst a bunch of fancy dressed fools. Them society folk don't want the likes of us in their ranks, Laura. You'll get hurt and so will that fool of a mother of yours." She stopped smiling at her; the concern on her face appeared to be genuine.

"Annie, there are good and bad in all ranks of society. Have you seen Pa?" Laura asked, moving the conversation on.

"Well, I've heard him. He was in the inn and you could clearly hear him singing from out here on the beach."

"But Pa can't sing, Annie, he drones," Laura said and smiled.

"That's how I knew it was him." Annie grabbed her hand as she had done so many times when they were children. They ran between the cobles, by the lobster pots, crab reels and stacked nets to the window of the inn. The shutters were open wide as the evening was windless and warm. They crouched and listened to the doleful wallow of a sea shanty, telling a tale of life and loss, in Obadiah's flat and toneless voice. They tried to peek through the crack of the shutter.

"That's, Pa," Laura whispered. "He has not improved any, has he? How long has he been down here?"

"Since he came back from the boats this afternoon he's been in there most of the time. Oh, he stopped long enough to see his 'lady friend' for dinner and then returned here. Looks like the honeymoon is finally over," Annie said, with more than a little look of satisfaction on her face.

They both stopped talking and leaned against the wall of the inn, listening keenly as voices raged on inside.

"For God's sake, man! What are you wallowing down here for when you have three good women up there?" Angus shook his head. Fortunately there was no other customers in the tap room.

"That's my pa shouting now!" Annie said. "What's he storming on about?"

Laura shrugged.

"Three good women? You do not know the half of it, man." Obadiah's voice slurred his reply. "Laura ain't no woman, she's still a child…"

"I do not mean Laura, you idiot." Angus sounded as though his frustration had reached his limit.

"Watch your tongue, Angus." Obadiah threw a punch that narrowly missed his friend's jaw. Angus grabbed Obadiah by the collar and spun him around, sending him out the front doorway of the inn and onto the beach. Now there was no need to peer around shutters, for the two young women had a clear view of what was happening.

"Listen and listen good. You have your posh wench settled into that hotel of yours, your wife in the new house, and my Ivy up there with her. Have you no shame, man? Your past, present, and future women all neat in one place until the present one, the good wife, leaves you. Then the past one can return to me and my Annie ... whilst you play Lord Muck with your future wench. What more do you want, another younger one? You're not a young catch anymore, man, and you're turning into an old drunken fool who could lose all of them." Angus stood with hands on his hips, oblivious to Laura and Annie's presence.

"Your Annie?" Obadiah questioned as he swayed in the breeze.

"Aye, mine from before she was born, so don't even go there, Obadiah, or I'll cut you down in pieces. Go home, to whichever one will have you, and send my wife back here to me. I love and need her and I am not ashamed to say it."

Obadiah was going to answer, but Annie's dazed figure stood forward. "Pa, whatever do you mean? Of course I am yours..." she said.

Angus rubbed his head with his hand and looked at Obadiah. "Go! Before I lame you," he shouted to him.

Obadiah hesitated for a moment until Laura stepped forward. She too looked pale and put her hand on Annie's arm.

"Later, Laura," Annie said and half smiled. "Take him to his whore. I need to go home with my pa." Angus's eyes were watering but he wrapped his arm around his daughter and walked her off the beach to their small and humble home.

Laura stood before Obadiah, so she had a half-sister, is that what the two meant? Her father had slept with Ivy as well? Good grief, was he totally made of immoral fibre? She had thought him strong but he did not have the backbone to stand by his mistakes, past or present. If he had she would not exist, but how could she ever look Annie in the eye again when their lives had been separated by her father's actions and greed. Obadiah was rubbing his eyes, still swaying. She reached into one of the cobles, fetched out an empty pail and filled it with sea water before throwing it at his face. He screamed an obscenity at her but sobered up somewhat.

"Hell, you are a witch at times!" he said.

"Annie, Ivy's daughter is my..."

"Let it go," he said and began walking to the bank.

"Let it go? She is my half-sister and you dismiss it, dismiss her from your life as you have Ma and me?" Laura quickened her pace so that she stood in front of him on the steep slope.

"I'm not the first or the last man who sought to have it all. I love you, wanted your ma's approval for what I did and the warmth of my Myrtle. I never saw it as a way of preventing the family from going on to better things. It was just ... convenient," he said.

"Mrs King is not one to be thought of as convenient, Pa, and neither is Ma. They deserve better. Ivy got lucky, she has a man who knows her past and still adores her. You have seen so much in your vision of the future of this town yet you failed to see what was in front of you: the people whose love you took for granted. Pa, we will leave, Ma and me, but for once in your life cherish just one woman, the one you are with, and treat her well, for if you do not you will have a lonely and sad future."

"When did you become so wise?" he asked, as he took hold of her hand.

"When I grew up. When I was nearly killed by a bullet from a gun on a land that I should never have set foot on. When I met a man who I would like to get to know, but who no longer desires to know me, and when I saw a young lad running for his life and helped him. When I realised my father was human and not made as a saint, with all the human frailty and faults that being one entails."

"Daniel is busy, Laura. He is learning about the work that we do for the Home Office. They are things that do not concern you, but that will ultimately stop this country from heading into a Luddite-driven revolution to mirror that of the France." He sighed and looked around. His voice was very low.

"Next you will claim that you work for the government!" She shook her head as she replied.

"In a way, I do." He almost looked proud to say it.

"You were a smuggler," she whispered.

"Aye, back in the day, but now, I, like a few others, listen and report back to the magistrate, to tell him of the unrest that has spread out of Lancashire. When they threatened to bring the Yeomanry Cavalry here I stepped up to the mark, but Daniel Tranton knew nothing of this because we needed him as bait. He is a good man and his mill is one of the best that has been seen, so they should, if genuine, have left him alone, but these men preach sedition and want anarchy. I helped bring them down and I would do it again."

Laura shook her head. "How complex your world is, Pa. Don't say I would not understand, for I understand treachery and betrayal well. You must put all right with Angus for he is the best friend you will ever have and you need him. Make amends with Ivy and provide for Annie, for she too deserves a good husband and a life of her own. If you know where Mr Daniel Tranton is then you tell him that I will not wait forever.

If he wants me he must prove it, and if he does not, then Pa, I will take Ma and that chaise down to Brighton to see how a resort on the south coast succeeds so well."

"That you will not!" he snapped.

Laura had had enough of arguing for one night and stormed up the hill back to her temporary home.

Chapter 13

Mrs Myrtle King rose early, as always. Her maid had already set the fires and made breakfast for her two guests. It was true what Gladys Pennington had said, as a business concern the hotel was pitiful, but she could see how the rooms could be used for the salt treatments on the ground floor to the rear of the building. There were all sorts of contraptions being invented to help cure people, but what of the age-old benefits of fresh seawater?

Then, for those of a stronger constitution, they could have trips down the bay to use the bathing machines, but the temperatures here were not as conducive as those on the south coast, so she thought that Obadiah's idea would only work for a few short months in summer. He thought like a hardened fisherman and not like the refined folk of the city, who were used to being closeted away in parlours and assembly rooms. However, if they made the most of indoor indulgences, then the place could become renowned. The views here were spectacular.

Mrs King made her way through the kitchen, checking that all was well with the cook and kitchen maid, but saw Jeb sitting on a wall outside. He was staring over at the boats by the inn.

Instantly her heart felt lighter, for with Obadiah's self-pitying mood her own had dampened slightly. Jeb, though, never failed to make her smile. "Hello, young man," she said and her heart lifted as his face turned to her with his usual happy greeting.

"Morning, Mrs King," he said and jumped down onto his feet.

"Here." She offered him a fresh bun, collected that morning from the bake house. That was something else that she wanted to talk to Obadiah about. It was small and covered the basics, but she wanted to expand it and have another oven installed so that cobs and loaves could be made to meet the extra demand if Gladys Pennington's ambitions paid off. If Ivy was staying in Ebton, then perhaps the woman would consider helping her. She would have to be careful how she broached these ideas to Obadiah — when he was sober would be a start!

"What were you watching, Jeb?" she asked.

"Just dreaming, Mrs King," he said, and his manner saddened. "Of what could be, and what will be," he added.

"Are you sure it was not a nightmare if it makes you look so pensive?" she asked and stood next to him. He suited the new trousers, boots, shirt and waistcoat that she had purchased for him. When he was washed and fed like he was when in her care, Myrtle King saw that he was a fine-looking lad. The shadows under his eyes had gone and the pink fresh skin that replaced his previously wan look suited him well.

"It's just, well, I saw that Mr Daniel Tranton ride down to the inn this morning. He was talking to Mr Pennington and that means…" He sighed and without thinking Mrs King placed a protective arm around his shoulder. She had never thought it possible to become so fond of a child in such a short time. She had seen him bloom. He leant his head against her side.

"I love it here," he said. "I hate them mills. I feel like I cannot breathe and the noise it drives my mind mad. I just want to run and run and run…"

Mrs King hugged him to her and fought the urge to allow the unshed tears to roll down her cheeks, for she did not want to lose him. The sense of loss and abandonment that his departure would bring her threatened to undermine her normally composed nature.

"Then we have a problem," Daniel Tranton's voice broke through her thoughts, but she felt Jeb's arm grip her waist tightly.

"No, we don't, sir. I was talking out of turn. You saved me," Jeb said. He let go of her and stood apart. "I know you have my papers and I'll honour them. It's just that I like the sea and open spaces better." He looked up at Mrs King. "When I've served my time, I'll come back here, Mrs," he said to her and she smiled.

"No you won't, lad," Obadiah's voice announced as he leaned against the back-door frame.

"Obadiah, please!" Mrs King stepped forward and put both her hands on Jeb's shoulders. "Let him have his dreams, Obadiah. You have always had yours."

"Obadiah and I have come to an arrangement," Daniel interrupted and explained. "I have transferred the lad's papers to him. He will go out on the boats and feel the salty air on his face. He is no use to me in the mill. His fear of the moving parts is too great. I think that if he returns he could cause himself injury and my machines damage — unintentionally. So there is no point in making him when he clearly is better suited to a life on the waves, helping Obadiah build his kingdom."

Jeb ran forward and hugged Daniel, who looked completely taken aback.

"I understand there are plans for a busier hotel here and that will also require more hands. I can speak for a young woman who knows her letters and numbers who is wasted serving where she is now. If you could do with extra help I will fetch her when next I return." Daniel winked at Jeb; whose quick wit had already realised who he was talking about.

"May?" Jeb asked. "You would rescue her also?"

Daniel nodded. "I think rescue is rather an exaggerated word. Perhaps help her make a better life for herself that she clearly deserves."

"She's like me sister," Jeb said and turned to Mrs King with wide hopeful eyes.

"Then we shall find good work for her, too," Mrs King said.

Obadiah stepped forward. "Daniel, you need to speak to Laura, and soon. She has got it into her head that you have lost interest in her because of her family's failings."

"You know that I have had to sort things out with Roderick." He shrugged.

"If he wants a good woman I know where there is one who would happily look after him. My Annie should not waste her life in the village…"

"Obadiah!" Mrs King snapped. "She is Angus and Ivy's Annie. Stop interfering."

"I will leave you now. I should have sent word to Laura but was swept away by the turn of events." Daniel nodded at Mrs King and left.

"Obadiah, you are sober," Mrs King remarked. Jeb ran out of the back gate and down the lane towards the beach. She realised he was avoiding what could be another argument between them. Obadiah had been argumentative and grumpy for two weeks and she had had quite enough of his moods.

"You want me to apologise?" he said.

"No, Obadiah, I do not. Your behaviour has been found wanting by many. There are too many apologies to make so just amend your ways. You have wallowed long enough. What I want you to do is to invest in the bakery and listen to my designs for some saltwater treatment rooms in the hotel."

"You women don't want much, do you?" he said and hugged her to him.

"No, not much," she said and kissed his grizzled cheek.

Daniel waited a while before venturing to the house to see Laura. He could not quite find the right words for what he wanted to say to her. They simply would not flow smoothly in his mind. He had become very fond of Laura, but the events with Roderick had turned his world upside down. To discover Roderick had been operating in a clandestine business with Pennington, forming a group of spies amongst the mill workers to weed out those who would spread violence was a lot to take in.

Daniel stared out at the magnificent headland of Stangcliffe; the sun cast its majestic rays upon its ruggedness; light and shade dramatically contrasted, as in life, ever changing. Cruel, greedy mill owners had treated their workers like slaves. He had seen this for himself when he visited the vast manufactories in Manchester. There was need for change, but not by violence, not by killing and destruction. The war had done too much of that. The conflicts had taken their toll on man and country alike. People were tired and many poor to the point of starvation. He would run their mills, Roderick's and his own, in a way that treated the workers fairly. Roderick was moving to London, to work in a government office.

How then to approach Miss Laura Pennington, a headstrong, attractive young lady who was someone he would like to have at his side throughout the vision he had? It was now or never, so as the two elder women walked along the top promenade, he approached her door and lifted the knocker. The door opened before he allowed it to fall.

"Mr Tranton, how good of you to call," Laura said, as she stepped back so that he could enter.

"I trust it is not at an inconvenient time?" He stepped inside.

"No, in fact, as you have seen my mama and her companion leave the house I would say that your timing is perfect. Come and talk to me."

Laura closed the door and walked into the day room. Daniel followed, closing the door behind them.

"Laura, I wish to be honest with you," he said.

"That is always a good place to start, Daniel, is it not?" She smiled.

"I have had much to think about these last few weeks. My eyes have been blinkered to some home truths that I failed to see and now they are open."

He paused. Laura looked at him and he realised that he was not making sense to her.

"Meaning what precisely?" she asked.

"I would like us to become engaged and announce it immediately. Then you will know how serious I am about you and making our union work." He watched her eyes widen and saw what he hoped was a favourable glint in them.

"You are proposing marriage to me?" she asked.

"Yes, before I ask your father officially and it is made known. If you still find the idea acceptable," he said and looked at her gentle smile. How he longed to kiss those lps and embrace her to show her how much he meant what he said.

"Daniel…" she began.

"I know I have acted like an arrogant fool in the past, but I am not that man. I want a good future for my workers and, of course, for us."

"Daniel…" Laura tried to speak again.

"Do not worry about Roderick for he is a changed man. He would not have hurt the boy…"

"Daniel!" she snapped. "Please let me speak."

He swallowed and nodded.

"Your past is your own. I am only interested in the present and the future. Our future, to be shared by us both."

"You are sure…" he began, but Laura stepped in front of him and those lips were so close that he stopped speaking and kissed her, tenderly at first but then with increasing urgency, half expecting her to strike his cheek or to push him away, but she did neither. Her arms encircled his neck and her body rose on tiptoe until he felt her warmth resting on him. Once parted, she looked up at him with more than a glint in her eyes, there was the undeniable spark of love and desire.

"Does that answer your question, Daniel?" she asked, and stepped back. "I do not see you as blinkered. I do not see you as a way out of the mess my family has become. I see you as a man with a vision, one that I share."

Daniel took both of her hands in his. "Then we shall ask your father straight away and let the world know." He moved forward but she stood still.

"No, Daniel. You asked me, I have given you my reply, now we will tell my father. He wanted this marriage match, but it is between us, not on his terms. Take nothing he offered, for I will come to you on my own, not as part of a bargain. He has lost the right to stand in my way or act as a 'broker'. I do not wish or need his blessing anymore." She looked away.

"Can you not forgive him?" Daniel asked her, as he entwined her fingers in his.

"In time, but our time is now, his is past, as far as his wife and daughter are concerned. He has left a legacy of broken relationships and I will not have him involved in ours."

"Very well." Daniel wrapped his arm around her. "Then let our own legacy begin right here and right now."

A NOTE TO THE READER

Dear Reader,

Thank you for choosing to read *To Have and To Hold*. I hope you enjoyed following Laura and Daniel as they rescued young Jeb and unearthed a group of mill agitators.

The Inspiration

Laura and Daniel change and learn important life lessons both about judging people and accepting their own failings as their relationship grows.

Laura idolised her father, Obadiah Pennington. He had taken his family's fortunes from the harsh life of a local fisherman to that of a successful businessman along the bay of Ebton. He is also a celebrated local hero. Obadiah's quick thinking fifteen years earlier prevented the coastal village burning to the ground, destroying the livelihood of all the villagers. This fire was started by the notorious leader of a gang of smugglers who featured in To Love, Honour and Obey.

Laura's image of her father is shattered. He proves to be only human with all the frailties that entails and her eyes are opened for the first time to see how her frustrated, bitter mother has suffered within a lonely ill-matched marriage. Yet the woman has so much potential when the opportunity to use it arrives.

Daniel Tranton is headstrong and a good mill owner believing in treating his workforce fairly for the times they lived in. His cousin Roderick appears to be a firmer, harsher mill owner, but he has a hidden agenda. Daniel is forced to see that his own arrogance has treated his relative unjustly in the past.

The Early Nineteenth Century

The 'Peterloo Massacre', in Manchester, happened a month prior to the setting of this story. It shocked the nation as the cavalry charged into a crowd of thousands of people meeting to protest about the appalling working conditions within the mills of West Yorkshire. Eighteen people died and hundreds were injured. Mistrust between the mill workers, the mill owners and the authorities was high as paid spies fed information back about gatherings.

Prior to the mills, weaving had been a cottage industry. With automation came a massive change to the local communities. The greed of the owners and poor working conditions caused poverty and injury to many.

After the Napoleonic wars unemployment was high, which meant labour was desperate and cheap. A child could be indentured, or apprenticed to a mill, for a set number of years and was subjected to the mill owners' whim. Jeb ran and was hunted by Ivor Bullman, a bully who thrived as a cruel foreman in my fictitious mill.

Fairer mill owners did exist, such as at, Quarry Bank Mill, Styal, Cheshire where the apprentices were given a basic education and sustenance.

The early nineteenth century was a period of great conflict and change: a time of war, pressgangs, and extreme social, agricultural, religious and political changes. All these impacted on the ordinary people who were left behind, whilst the wars with Napoleon dragged on.

The countryside was changing as mills were being built and cottage industries suffered, along with their communities. The population gravitated to these places of work and life in the countryside changed.

My Ebton had a history of smuggling. The government taxed its people harshly, whilst still fearing the possibility of a revolution as had happened in France. It was hardly surprising then that smuggling and opportunists abounded, yet in plying the trade they gave coin to an enemy. Some gangs were known for their violence, others were less so and merely supplied a ready market that crossed over social rank and was often funded by a moneyed man.

With the onset of the Industrial Revolution, Luddite activities and the growth of new money, lives were changing and the old money was feeling threatened.

In the cities 'society' had strict rules: influence and connections were so very important.

In my books the settings are more remote. These influences mean nothing when a character is dealing with survival, either their own, or someone who they have met. So boundaries are crossed, rules of society are broken or are made irrelevant.

The Region

Most of my titles are set in an area of the country that I love: North Yorkshire, with its beautiful coast and moors.

To Have and To Hold begins in Ebton. This is based on the well known Victorian town of Saltburn-by-sea, North Yorkshire.

I used my fictitious market towns of Beckton and Gorebeck both having their own small mills situated just outside the towns.

The essence of The Yorkshire Saga series:

Love is a timeless essential of life. Throughout history, love in all its forms is a constant: be it passionate, caring, needy, manipulative, possessive or one that is strong enough to cross barriers of culture or faith. When two souls meet in a situation which takes them out of their normal social strata or into a shared danger, a relationship forms as the adventure unfolds.

If you enjoyed reading *To Have and To Hold* I would really appreciate it if you could take a moment to leave a review either on **Amazon** or **Goodreads**, or wherever you wish.

It is always helpful to read feedback and I am always interested in what my reader's think, or would like to read next.

I can be contacted on:-

Facebook: **ValerieHolmesAuthor**

Twitter: **@ValerieHolmesUK**

Or through my website: **www.ValerieHolmesAuthor.com**

Love the Adventure!

Valerie Holmes

Sapere Books is an exciting new publisher of brilliant fiction and popular history.

To find out more about our latest releases and our monthly bargain books visit our website:
saperebooks.com

Printed in Great Britain
by Amazon